# The Dance of Geometry

# Brian Howell

## The Dance of Geometry

*The* Toby Press

First Edition 2002

*The* Toby Press *LLC*

www.tobypress.com

Copyright © Brian Howell, 2002

The right of Brian Howell to be identified as the author of this work has been asserted by him in accordance with the Copyright, Designs & Patents Act 1988

All rights reserved. No part of this publication may be reproduced, stored in a retrieval system or transmitted in any form or by any means, electronic, mechanical, photocopying or otherwise, without the prior permission of the publisher, except in the case of brief quotations embodied in critical articles or reviews.

This is a work of fiction. The characters, incidents, and dialogues are products of the author's imagination and are not to be construed as real. Any resemblance to actual events or persons, living or dead, is entirely coincidental.

ISBN 1 902881 47 8, *hard cover*
ISBN 1 902881 48 6, *paperback*

A CIP catalogue record for this title is available from the British Library

Cover Illustration, *The Music Lesson* by Johannes Vermeer. Reproduced with the permission of The Royal Collection © 2001, Her Majesty Queen Elizabeth II

Designed by Breton Jones, London

Typeset in Garamond by
Rowland Phototypesetting Ltd., Bury St Edmunds, Suffolk, England

Printed and bound in the United States by
Thomson-Shore Inc., Michigan

*For Chizue, Kai, and Jenna*

"The illusion which he seeks is not closeness but distance . . . Immediacy, touch, are excluded; his subject is the immutable barrier of space"

*Lawrence Gowing:* Vermeer *(Giles de la Mare, 1952)*

## Contents

Part one: *Johannes*     1

Part two: *The Shifting Surface of Desire*     81

Part three: *Reconstruction*     153

Part four: *The Shifting Surface of Desire (reprise)*     193

# Part one:
## *Johannes*

*Chapter one*

His father had always been two persons, but only when Reynier took his son one day to the market on business did Johannes become aware of this second person, the one who was attempting to impart knowledge to the eight-year-old.

A passing trader, a stranger to Reynier, had set up with an assortment of wares, among these the silk known as caffa. Johannes noticed how Reynier caught the man's eye, how his father's hand delved into the folds of the material he knew so well. The boy was not supposed to touch but did so, oblivious to censure.

'Johannes!' Reynier warned.

Johannes continued to worry the cloth. He had known the feeling before, but this time his investigation took a different form, one that tried to follow the pattern that one moment was there, the next not.

He looked up at his father. He was seeing him, too, in a new light; his body was now a contradiction, a bulky torso like a bursting sack of grain, short legs that more than matched the power and threat of the upper half, and the hands. These hands were huge like his own, and till now were the only ones in the family to caress the merchants' silks, to make their invisible inventory of warp and weft as they assessed texture. These same hands were capable of hoisting barrels or suspending the child's life over an ocean of fear should he swerve from the path that was good. Yet Reynier never hit his child; there had never been occasion.

'Two guilders.' Reynier gave the trader's offer some thought, then, on the point of turning, decided to buy the cloth.

Johannes recognised the change in Reynier: during the walk home, his father was suddenly taken with explaining the details of the material, how it was made, its advantages over other cloths. Johannes had never known him quite so forthcoming.

As there were two fathers, there were two worlds, indoors and outdoors, and it often seemed that there was no connection between the two. The indoor world, which dominated, was defined by dark. Even inside was never completely inside, because line and form conspired to direct the eye into the deeper space. Doors led to other doors, pictures to other pictures; mirrors, which resembled pictures, threw the boy back from where he had come into another, framed world.

At the centre of the indoor world was the inn proper, where elegant forms, muffled by pipe smoke and whispers, would move in a blur to their customary positions, releasing an expression of thanks or even a coin to the young Johannes as he brought them their drinks.

Plain, thin-faced and still unmarried, his sister Gertruy would draw the men's attention, even the occasional officer's. Perhaps Reynier's vigilance over his male customers and his violent history made them keep their distance and lubricious glances within the purview of decorum. Perhaps his concern for his cherished painters led him to neglect her prospects. Yet their stares did not reach further than her goodness, her good intentions; they did not go beyond the skin into the gentle heart of her.

It was January three years before when they ran The Flying Fox in the Voldersgracht behind the Great Market Square. A wind from the sea is scything through the narrow streets of the town, and the ice by the woods is a closed eye which could at any moment open and swallow up the drifting, cheering forms. Reynier is sturdy, compact, thundering around on big skates, the best of the *kolf* players. A sudden collision, and three forms are on the ice in a clap of laughter, where they remain until a question is asked: where is Reynier?

In the near distance, by the trees, Reynier and another figure stand, knives glistening like lizards' tongues, and before Reynier's friends can draw themselves up, the other man is upon the innkeeper. Reynier's successful parries only inspire the assailant, and it is doubtful that Reynier will survive the attack. His friends gather around the attacker, who is not letting up, and they rain down on him with their kolf clubs until he is on the ice, his legs askew. Reynier is now restrained from what he considers a just retribution, and it takes all three of them to draw him away. In the inn, the cause of the altercation emerges: the culprit, a captain in the army, had commented on the reputation of the establishment Reynier kept and the rôle of his daughter, Gertruy. His friends laugh off the accusation for what it is: unfounded. And it seems that all is settled.

Yet late that night the five-year-old awakes to witness a scene that will remain indelible: his father on the stairs, much enraged by his own drink, being held back by Johannes' mother Digna and Gertruy. There is a knife, one the child has never seen before, its shiny edge seeming to jump out at the boy as the trio struggle as one—a maimed, purposeless beast. The sounds that they make, a melding of harsh commands, moans, and cooing, will stay in the boy's memory almost as long as the sight of the dagger. Yet they persuade him, finally, with arguments Johannes cannot follow, to abide by the law. And in the morning Reynier is his everyday self, as if nothing has taken place to perturb his ambitions for respectability.

The day they moved to the Mechelen inn on the Great Market Square, Johannes saw a new Delft. The Nieuwe Kerk and the Town Hall to either side, whilst never crowding out the unending sky, defined the narrow compass of his visible world. He need never leave the square again. No, he did not even wish to. He would be happy to go with his father forever to solemn meetings where documents were signed and expressions exchanged to an air of perfunctory civic satisfaction. Or to follow Gertruy to the market, her face dipped into its collar as if the attention she did not seek nor gain pushed her gaze inward.

It was on one of those early days after the move that he saw Catharina Bolnes for the first time too. She was standing with her mother and a gentleman, looking impatiently out of her bonnet as if to protest against the restricted view. Her mother's expression was severe but respectful to the man. Perhaps in that petulant swivel of hers the young girl saw Johannes for a moment, linked to his sorrowful sister as fast as she herself was to her mother.

Gertruy noticed his sudden lagging behind, and looked up for only the third or fourth time during their walk.

'Johannes, don't stare.'

'Who is she?'

'Maria Thins. Can't you see she's talking to that heretic priest?'

'No, not her, the . . .'

She let out a rare puff of irritation.

'Her daughter, Catharina, I should think. What do you want with her? They wouldn't talk to the likes of us, even if we converted.'

'Why should we convert?'

'Johannes!' Gertruy huffed, shaking her head, and pulled her brother along roughly.

That night the eight-year-old Johannes intimated what was to come. Although he could not name the thing itself, the whole, it was there in separated parts. Out of the darkness it took the form of an insoluble dream.

He was walking along a street in Delft behind two men who carried between them a large, heavy ebony frame whose parameters directed his attention towards a series of passing shapes and faces in the street. None of these was familiar until he saw the face of a woman, perhaps in her twenties, coming straight towards the frame, as if she would not stop. She walked up to him and stood looking through the frame, which was now angled forward as if to keep her in perspective while she looked down at him. Now the arms of the men holding the frame disappeared with the frame itself and she was leaning down at him, looking into his eyes. He no longer had the protective boundaries of the frame. He was out in the world. There was an intimation of a smile, but he could no longer be sure. His vision was misted up. He could not see her face. Standing on the corner of the street as he was, he felt lonelier than he had ever done in his life. Neighbourhood friends with whom he regularly scrapped in the market now passed him by, their eyes directed to the ground. He called but they ignored him. He woke up crying, as if those tears had stopped him seeing properly. Now he saw Gertruy. She had heard him and was leaning over him.

One evening Johannes was told to stop serving and go up to his father's workroom. The door was open. Silently, Johannes approached his father as he crouched in front of his loom. Before the boy could surprise him, Reynier stopped his weaving and turned around to reach for the sketches he had made in preparation. He handed them to Johannes. The boy's attention was equally divided between the drawn designs and the cloth.

'Which do you prefer?'

Johannes looked from Reynier to the drawing, then to the cloth, and back to his father.

'What do you want to be? A weaver, or an artist?'

Johannes' tentative finger reached towards the loom. Reynier showed no reaction. At the last moment, as if it were a game between father and son, Johannes chose the sketches, and giggled.

A year later Johannes made the first of his daily trips to the painter Cornelis Daemen Rietwijck's academy on the nearby Voldersgracht to learn drawing.

Then there was Digna. And her tales. Her stories of her brother, Balthens, and her father, Balthasar Gerrits, and their adventures interleaved his earliest days, sewing up the more languorous periods with imagined scenes of activity with which his young mind avidly colluded. Even when his mind and body were full of other things, the stories were always in the background somewhere, neither intrusive nor oppressive, but a presence of which he remained aware.

Johannes' grandfather and uncle had been counterfeiters. They had forged coins. Balthens had been thrown into prison, had been tortured, but he had risen above his misdeeds to become an inventor of machines used by the army to protect Holland from the wrath of the Spanish. Even now, at the endangered city of Sas van Gent, he was most probably engaged in invaluable work . . .

'He was not appreciated, your uncle, they would have killed him, his own *employers*, the States General that is, and sacrificed all Holland had it not been for the appearance of a mysterious stranger. I think that only that man, whoever he was, knew the value of your uncle's talents.'

One afternoon Reynier walked into the kitchen once more to hear his wife recounting the familiar story. He lost his temper and threw a faïence dish against the wall.

'What rubbish are you speaking again? Do you want the boy to grow up thinking he is descended from criminals?'

'Talented criminals at any rate,' she retorted as she picked up the pieces, keeping her eyes lowered.

At such moments Johannes felt their life to be as fragile as that ruined piece of crockery. And the feeling of potential destruction was all the keener as the child anticipated his mother's next words. She was afraid of Reynier, to be sure, but she would not hold back when she deemed her husband to be unjust. On this occasion Reynier did not give her the opportunity.

'He has all the talent he needs in those hands of his,' he said.

All three looked down at those broad wedges of flesh, which in their seeming awkwardness promised so little. At that moment Johannes looked up, smiled, and the heaviness in the air was broken. In the middle of this Gertruy walked into the room to find the trio laughing. Her smile, which was a beautiful one, also turned into a laugh.

Johannes had never seen anyone dressed like Rietwijck. At first the old man's breeches and long coat frightened him, but he was to become an ally. The other, older pupils, who read in his dress a liking for the French style, would sometimes hum a French tune, but Rietwijck's ability to locate the culprits and issue summary punishment seemed quite uncanny to Johannes. Impatient to draw, Johannes made slow progress in arithmetic, geometry, and astronomy. Yet his ability to absorb Aristotle and Alberti baffled the teacher.

After lessons, Gerrit, carrot-topped and muscular, and his brother Simon, blond and skinny, would try to block the younger apprentice's exit, lurching from one side of the alley to the other as Johannes ran their interweaving gauntlet. When they finally succeeded in snatching from Johannes' bag a sketch he had made of Mechelen, its size out of proportion to the other houses and the Nieuwe Kerk on the square, Gerrit and Simon sank down on the cobbled stones in peals of laughter. Their mockery hurt more than the worst of their thrashings.

The rug was draped across a table and a plate of fruit placed on it. Johannes' attention was held more by the pattern of the rug than by the light cast on the fruit. He was hungry. Once, Gerrit had taken a cluster of grapes, destroying the composition Johannes had laboured over for hours. Rietwijck had not noticed on that occasion.

Today Johannes had spent so long on the detail of the rug that the bowl had wandered to the edge of the table. Now he was faced with a mess.

The old man stood in disbelief as he looked at Johannes' work.

'What is that? It inhabits no space that I know of.'

It was true, he now saw.

Rietwijck continued his inspection of the others' work. 'Excellent, excellent, excellent.' Each phrase exploded a small bomb of humiliation within Johannes. I will never draw, I won't learn numbers, I hate numbers, he told himself sullenly, but his teacher returned to him and replaced the sheet. Rietwijck looked at his timepiece, then dismissed the others.

Gerrit and Simon hovered awhile, only reluctant to leave because the prospect of their after-lesson fun had been scotched. Rietwijck kept Johannes for another hour without charge until he had produced a satisfactory rendition.

The man was laid on the rack, his arms and feet extending to the four corners as if these supported the very construction. He was no longer whole yet his body had never felt so complete in its purpose. The sheriff gave the order for the 200-pound weights to be lowered, then lifted, and Johannes looked on, fixed as much by horror as by the ring of soldiers around his uncle. How would his uncle ever recover to save the nation? Did they not know about his talents?

The weights were lifted momentarily, only to be lowered once more, and Johannes heard in his uncle's scream the rush of cascading waves, which would engulf them all if the officials persisted in their unjust intentions. But the moans grew ever louder until they swallowed everyone in the room, and Johannes woke to the taste of his own sea-salty tears. Then Gertruy was there, comforting him. Through the gap he saw the half-open door and heard mocking voices from the inn downstairs.

'Who will save Uncle Balthens from the torture?' he implored, still half in his nightmare. 'Who will save Sas van Gent?'

'Torture? Uncle Balthens?' It was almost a laugh, but one tinged with irritation.

'Uncle Balthens was not tortured, it was an . . . acquaintance. And besides, there is news—Sas van Gent is saved. Holland is saved!'

Gertruy would not allow her tone to betray the anger she felt at her mother for filling the boy's head to such effect as this, nor to sour the relief that she shared with all those carousing downstairs whose raucous celebration had most probably contributed to her brother's feverish state.

'They are saved,' she allowed herself once more, kissing her brother on the cheek.

As she pulled up the bed linen about him, Reynier appeared at the door, blotting out the threshold like spilled ink. For a moment she had feared a drunken customer.

'Downstairs,' was all he said.

The night visions found their counterparts in a cluster of incidents that occurred shortly after the move to Mechelen, incidents that revolved around one memorable evening when he was helping Gertruy serve in the inn. Johannes had been aware that since the move a number of things had changed, some of them palpable, such as the addition of a painting in recent years, an old-fashioned merry company of elegant ladies and gentlemen, which Reynier had proudly hung behind the bar. And there was a distant relative, who had on occasion come to play the guitar. Other changes were harder to define.

Yet the usual combinations were present—the sweet smell of smoke that always stung his eyes, the trio of good-for-nothings who played cards and hunched over the coals of their tobacco pouches; two fishwives; the gentle frame maker, Anthony van der Wiel, Gertruy's suitor, along with his brothers; the local baker; Itge Jacobs and another woman. In short, the locals from the Fox, good and bad, had followed them to Mechelen.

That evening Johannes noticed some newer customers, a group of well-dressed young men, one of them a soldier. After his return to the inn from a short meal break, Johannes had good reason to study the man more closely. The soldier, who sat by the window, had his back turned away from Johannes. Sitting across the table from him, to the boy's astonishment, was Gertruy. The soldier's companions had shifted to the end of the table. As Johannes walked by them, the soldier's red jacket seemed to dominate everything else in the inn. Gertruy barely noticed her brother as he passed by with the tankards to the card players.

'Yes, and there'll be trouble yet,' he caught one saying.

'Soon he'll only let in the likes of them,' said another, tilting his head in the direction of the soldier and the well-dressed men.

It was the mood of the tavern that had changed. Johannes continued on to the fishwives. As he approached, they curtailed their talk abruptly, and gave their orders. They did not smile in their usual happy-go-lucky way. He went up to Itge, who, engrossed in her latest commentary on the state of the town's morals, did not notice his approach.

'Bits of flesh, they say, have fallen out of her . . . She'll not be stepping into any young man's house for a while, I shouldn't wonder.' As she saw him, she drew in her breath, and, puffed up like a pigeon, looked around with a self-satisfied expression. The other woman ordered sharply.

At the bar, waiting for the orders, he now saw the change more concretely. He became aware that there were not only fewer customers in the inn, but their composition, which normally presented itself as a single entity, albeit a raucous one, was now broken up. Limbs, the sway of bodies, the directions of people's gazes, were no longer harmonious. The place was taut with uncertainty. Yet Reynier and Digna showed no sign of being aware of this.

Johannes stood there for a moment, as if separated completely from this scene and yet somehow mocked by it. Why would Gertruy not look at him? Would the soldier take her away from Anthony, from the inn, from them all? He wanted to ask his mother, but he could not find the words.

Reynier noticed his son standing there motionless, wearing a fixed, wan look. Perhaps serving in the tavern was dulling his brain. Hardly looking at him, Digna passed her son two tankards. When he had served the beers, he went over to Anthony and his brothers. They too were mumbling with discontent.

'It's not true, I tell you. If you were my brothers, you would know that when I say it,' Anthony was declaring in a shrill voice. Despite this, he managed a smile for Johannes. This reassured the boy, but as he moved away, he heard Gertruy's name issue from one of them.

His hands shaking, and the empty glasses rattling, Johannes went up to his mother and buried his face in her chest. The realization had come suddenly, sweeping him away on a

wave of humiliation so that tears came and made his eyes burn even more than usual. 'What is it, son?'
'They're saying things about Gertruy.'
'No, what kind of things?'
'I don't know. Who is that man she is with?'
'That's the captain. He's a friend of ours.'
'What's she doing?'
'She's not working tonight, that's all.'

His fears were almost assuaged, almost beginning to disappear, when they were revived and given a definite form.

Itge Jacobs, now openly drunk, walked over to Gertruy and made her accusation public. Perhaps spurred on by the unusual attention that Gertruy was receiving from the captain, Itge began to fawn on the soldier, one minute falling against him, the other threatening immediately to fall back. This left the gentleman with no choice but to catch her by the arm.

'That's it, wonderful,' Itge said, surprisingly in control all of a sudden, 'you don't want to play with them that's had pieces . . .'

At this Anthony stood up in a rage, his older, bigger brothers holding him back with embarrassing ease. The fishwives displayed amused smiles.

'Enough!'

Reynier's exclamation thundered across the inn.

'Out, woman! Enough! This is a respectable house, and I will only serve those worthy of it.'

Reynier now took the drunken Itge by the arm and thrust her out onto the street. Inside, he turned and cast his eyes across the cowering company, pointed at Itge's companion, the fishwives, then at the card players.

'And you, and you, and you. Out. Respectable people only. This is an end to gossip. I have a business to run.'

The card players, the fishwives and the woman filed out sheepishly.

The only words he had after this were to his son: 'A beer to everyone in the house.'

Some days after that evening, Johannes accompanied his father to the notary, Willem de Langue. It was not the first time that he had been on this short trip, but the occasion gained a special place in his childhood.

They would normally have approached De Langue's via the Great Market Square, but on this day Reynier had picked Johannes up from Rietwijck's in the Voldersgracht and was intending to continue to the bottom of the street, thus avoiding going onto the crowded square. As they walked along the canal, he noticed how withdrawn his father was.

Johannes stopped to look at the tower of the Nieuwe Kerk, which seemed at this moment to lean and threaten to fall. He felt a need to go by the usual route, through the square. He reached out a hand, but Reynier was gone. He walked on to the corner, crying out for his father. Now, the buttresses of the church were like the sprung legs of a giant insect. Then, looking round, he saw Reynier coming out of the tailor's, shaking hands with the tradesman. Johannes ran, into his father's arms. Johannes pulled him back into the square.

'Johannes? What's the matter?'

'Why didn't you stop for me? The tower's falling.'

Reynier smiled. 'The tower falling, eh?' We'll see.'

They walked into the square, and stood looking up at the tower and its spire.

'You see? It's not falling, Johannes. As long as it's there, you know where you are. You know where north and south are.'

Johannes nodded, uncertain but calmed.

They walked to the other side of the square, where they turned left along the Oude Langendijck till they reached De Langue's office on the cattle market. The building was slightly wider than most in Delft, as if to suggest its importance over the adjacent residences. They were met by De Langue's secretary, who asked them to wait.

During this time, Johannes, thinking of the events in the inn, said, 'Father?'

'Yes, son.'

'Who was the soldier? Did he come for Gertruy?'

'Where did you get that idea from?'

'Anthony didn't look happy.'

Reynier cleared his throat, then reached for his handkerchief. Johannes noticed it was new and very white.

'He was . . . interested. You needn't worry yourself.'

'Will Gertruy marry Anthony?'

'In due course, Johannes, in due course.'

Johannes sat there, puzzled, but before he had a chance to pursue the subject, the secretary came out and ushered them in. As they entered there came polite mutterings indicating that a matter of great weight had finally been concluded.

Behind the desk stood the portly De Langue. His expression was stern but not impenetrable, and a stranger might have a detected a kindly disposition. Around the desk, in addition to his father and the notary, as if radiating unequally from the document placed there, stood three figures, all of whom Johannes had seen in the inn. The man who stood nearest to the document and signed first was addressed by De Langue as Jan Baptist van Fornenburgh, and was followed in turn by Pieter Anthonisz. van Groenewegen and Balthasar van der Ast, then finally, by Reynier.

Johannes held on to his father's hand and watched how slowly, how thoughtfully, he signed, 'Reynier Jansz. Vermeer, alias Vos.'

A small chuckle went round the group as they saw the boy shadow his father with curiosity.

On the way home, Johannes attempting to keep up with

his father's enlivened step, asked, 'What does it mean? Are we now called Vermeer, father?'

Reynier stopped suddenly, and lowered himself so that his head was level with his son's, and he grasped hold of the boy, revelling in the diminutive mirror of his own jutting jaw and wide mouth that seemed so open, so impressionable.

'Yes, it means we have made a change. We are now Vermeer or, if you wish, van der Meer. We are of the lake. Our fate is linked with water like that of the seven States. And,' he glanced in the direction of The Flying Fox inn nearby, 'we have moved from that place. For good.'

The days with Rietwijck sank under a vast perse cloud weighed down with numbers, lines, triangles, projections. He was not a prize pupil. He forced himself to adequacy. He did not understand, yet he was fascinated, and perhaps it was this that tempered Rietwijck's otherwise impatient nature. And Johannes' drawing had improved little. At one stage he had been in danger of being overtaken even by slow Adriaen, the clumsy, heavyset youth whose job it was to clean the brushes . . . whom Rietwijck kept on more out of pity than for any other reason.

One day Johannes asked the other boy if he enjoyed the simple act of pulverising pigments, Adriaen responded with the words, 'Yes, I see things in them.'

When Johannes asked him exactly what it was that he saw, Adriaen simply said, 'Beautiful, coloured monsters.'

Despite the oddness of such statements, which for Adriaen were not untypical, Johannes had formed a friendship with this boy, who lived in the house, and this gave Johannes justifiable occasion to stay awhile after the lessons. It was on one of these occasions that Johannes took to browsing through Rietwijck's modest library.

There were perhaps twenty books in all, mostly in Latin. He could by now decipher the titles and purposes of most of these, and one quarto volume, which had the word FRISIO in gold lettering on the spine, caught his attention. Rietwijck, who was involved in a complicated operation to repair the blinds, looked around momentarily to see the young boy stretching for this book on one of the higher shelves. Rietwijck was about to help him, but Johannes succeeded in inching it out until it fell into the safety of his grasp. His moustache twitching with curiosity at Johannes' precocity, Rietwijck decided to say nothing, seeing that the book was undamaged. As his pupil became quietly lost in the network of diagrams and engravings, the master recognised the book immediately: De Vries' *Perspective*.

The teacher observed the boy's raptness. He recalled his own first perusal of the book, in his youth. It had been as if he had entered a strange world where everything that was subject to definition by straight lines was demonstrated. A grid of boxes or tiles was always the measure of space and proportion, whether it was a room, a square, or some architectural fancy. Where points could be connected to the horizon they were connected, and these joined at eye level in beautiful harmony; even rounded figures were subject to these lineal concentrations and convergences.

Rietwijck noticed where Johannes' gentle turning of the pages had come to a halt; he knew that he could cough or cast a shadow across the boy and it would not disturb him. What could his pupil make of this drawing, an example of two distance points, which flanked a central vanishing point? He was tempted to question the boy, but decided to let his enjoyment of such work remain innocent. There would be time. He left the boy on his own and went off to light the candles in the rest of the downstairs rooms.

Johannes continued to study the network of diamond tiles demonstrated in the diagram until there was barely any light to see by, even when he went over to the window. But there was enough for him to notice when he came across another engraving that he had overlooked at the very beginning of the book. Soon after that, he fell into a deep sleep.

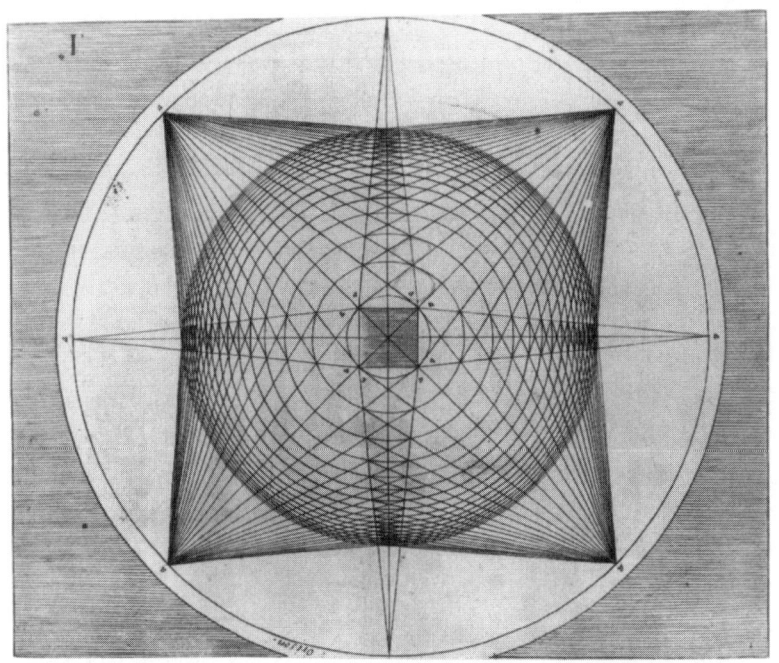

*Orbital diagram of the visual field, from Hans Vredeman de Vries'*
Perspective, *The Hague and Leiden, 1604–5*

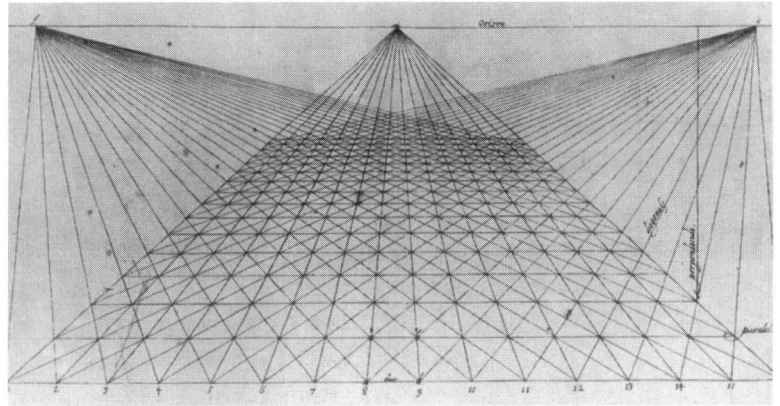

*Basic perspective construction using two 'distance points' from*
*Vredeman de Vries'* Perspective

The eye pulsed and swirled about a hidden axis. Pyramids radiated about its centre and travelled to the four corners, held down by fixed points, as if to form a buckled, imperfect canvas. These were areas of peripheral vision, and they were pinned down by the intersecting cross of one sharp, demanding focus, where what was seen was overwhelming. In the swirl of scenes—knife on flesh, blood on ice, restricting bars, the warm, comforting bosom of his mother—his thoughts floated away, and swam to the edge of vision once more.

Rietwijck's gentle pat on the back brought him suddenly out of the flood of thoughts. 'We shall make a painter of you yet, though it will not be within my time with you.'

Johannes, sleepy as he still was, found it hard to pay attention, and his teacher seemed disappointed by the boy's lack of response to the compliment.

'Now, boy, go. You have work to do in the tavern.'

By the end of the year Rietwijck's simple instruction gave way to that of two local masters, and it seemed that nothing would come of the months spent poring over the book by De Vries and another by Dürer. The first of his mentors, Evert van Aelst, showed little interest in him beyond doing what was necessary to repay the debts he had accumulated in Reynier's inn. He already had his favourites, and his world was as distant and ungraspable as the still lifes at which he excelled.

The apprenticeship did not outlast the debt, and not even the acquisition of one of Van Aelst's paintings, which Reynier could not sell, could satisfy the innkeeper. Sensing Johannes' mute protest, Reynier decided to take on the extra expense of another master. The impending transition was not a smooth one, and knowledge of it came to the young artist in the form of another dispute.

Johannes arrived back at the inn already shaken. For the

second time he had seen her, and his stomach was unsettled with anxiety. This time she had appeared even haughtier than the first, but she was not with her mother; the lady who accompanied her was perhaps her aunt. Had she seen him? He could not know. Her custom of casting her eyes down was more pronounced than before, but he had time to register the deep-set sockets of her eyes and her broad features. He had rarely seen anyone of his own age of such bearing and dressed in such manner except in the finest paintings. She already wore a jacket and dress of material the like of which his father had never woven. And Gertruy certainly did not possess clothing of such quality.

It seemed the source of the dispute was not financial.

In the main kitchen Digna sat with her hands dipped between her large thighs. Johannes entered, catching her in mid-sentence, so light was his tread.

'. . . because the man's a Catholic, and that will be the ruination of our son.'

'What rot you talk, woman. Even Rembrandt had a Catholic master.'

'Yes, and look at the result?'

'Result? When did you see a Rembrandt?'

She turned her face to the light, the sun's stencil of lattice casting a stretched diamond of deep blue across her apron.

'I have heard,' she answered almost under her breath.

'Heard,' Reynier repeated contemptuously. 'It's the first I've heard you know anything about art.'

'I can remember days when you talked of nothing else, even weaving. Don't you think that I wanted to learn more?' She paused awhile for breath, then went on, 'Reynier, do you want your son to hide his talents behind this . . . these . . . biblical . . .' she waved her arm in a wide circle, grasping for the word, 'these biblical . . . whatnots?'

'Listen, Digna, we're talking about the training. That's basic to every artist. Bramer can guarantee that.'

'If my father . . .'

At this dawning of an old argument, Reynier's body tensed, so that his stumpy muscles showed momentarily through his shirt, his whole frame seeming to prepare for some impact.

It was only now that they became aware of the child, standing in the oblong of shadow cast by the half-open door, through the low, consistent waves of sound which were for all his attempt to cover them unmistakable: their son had heard everything and was standing there crying.

From the bottom of the Great Market, he ran along the canal, then cut across a bridge, to the south of the town, then another bridge, the light fading all the while. He did not dare to look back.

He continued through the last quarter of houses until he reached the town wall. Though there was the wall, he could cross a bridge into open fields. Where was he to go? There was no mystery beyond this point. He knew where he was when he saw the towering windmill by the Schiedam Gate. He had rarely visited the harbour except with his mother or father, and he had been warned of its dangers: of the tides that would suddenly engulf the wharf, sweeping away hapless children; of unscrupulous men who would take a child on board a ship, never to be seen again; of the women who patrolled the area for no respectable reason.

There was little light from the street lanterns here, but a ship was being loaded. A middle-aged man was overseeing the work, and a woman was walking by, glancing at the men as she passed by them. Then she returned, and did the same again. After some time, when the stevedore seemed to be happy with his men, she approached him, not saying a word. He spent some time assessing her, then took her by the arm, pulling harshly.

Johannes drew back into the shadow of the Gate, where

he had been standing till now. There was a knowing laugh in the distance from the sailors, along with a few envious grunts. He almost fell backwards when he realised that the stevedore was coming towards the Gate with the woman. He drew further back into the shadow, holding his breath.

The man stopped and pushed her against the wall. They hadn't seen him. The woman demanded money, and with a barely suppressed groan he passed some coins to her. Johannes could see nothing. He wanted to leave but knew that were he to move now, he might be thought to be spying on them, held up to ridicule in front of the whole ship, or perhaps even taken away.

He heard cloth rip, then the rising and falling tones of the two invisible figures scarcely four feet from him, the sound of rough cloth against rougher brick, the man's sudden snort and a final bluster and sigh. All the while Johannes tried to summon up the image of Catharina, as if in an act of repudiation, but only the barest outline appeared. Then this moment of seeming calm was broken by the sound of a thump like a hand hitting a sack of grain, as Johannes heard the woman slump down to the ground and the man walked off, adjusting his breeches.

'Bastard,' he heard her mutter as she tried to stifle tears, then quite beyond his belief, she said, 'I know you're there, love. Don't be afraid.'

Johannes started to move away, gradually but determinedly. When he was perhaps ten feet out, she emerged, her bodice hanging limply where it had been torn. He could not make out the colour in the light. But not even the brief sight of her full, milky-white breasts could divert his eyes away from her face, a beautiful one, distorted only by ridges of red around her eyes, cheeks, and mouth.

He walked on for twenty yards, in a haze of shame and pity, at one point almost stumbling down the bank into the canal. As he pulled himself up, he stumbled into something hard and abrasive, smelling of sweat, and started to run before he even thought to look up. But a hand had caught him by the wrist.

Slowly, the realisation came, the familiar touch, the attractive force that brought him round as if he were one celestial body in the thrall of another. He was staring at the moon face of his father where argent tears had welled in the corners of his eyes. Hand in hand, they walked in silence back to the inn, the son's mind playing back this unlikely sequence of events. The subject of the evening's argument was smothered by welcoming relief. Of the encounter Johannes had witnessed, he could and would say nothing except to Gertruy.

## Chapter two

He left Van Aelst's indifferent tutelage with little regret, sensing that it had been motivated solely by that master's need to make good his alcoholic indulgences. But there remained some apprehension of who and what would take his place.

Reynier was absorbed by the triple task of running the inn, dealing in paintings, and weaving ever greater consignments of caffa. The boy sometimes feared for his father, so consumed with the latter, that the fabric of his being might never be separated from the very weave, and the man lost forever to the subtle intertwining of colour and line. Yet there was hardly time for pity or even contemplation. For six months there was no talk of drawing—the whole family was turned like heated metal to the purpose of building up Mechelen's trade.

On those few occasions he was allowed to pass by Rietwijck's or Van Aelst's houses, entrance to them was barred, if not outright, then by their preoccupation with their current, more fortunate pupils. Access to Rietwijck's library was the sorer of the two debarments; it had became his secret mission, to possess one day those pictures of fine perspectival networks which seemed to glue themselves and get entangled in his thoughts. It was a dream that he could not even impart to Gertruy. And when he passed Van Aelst's studio he would sometimes catch sight of the same pupils he had studied with, envying even the chore of grinding colours. But he pulled himself away from bitterness.

It was 1644. Johannes would soon reach thirteen, and the issue of his next teacher had still not been settled. Reports of the States' progress stole into town from the unlikeliest sources. Whales had been beached in continuous formations that suggested Holland was well fortified against floods either of water or the onslaughts of the Spanish; a beggar woman had seen a cloud weighted with blood. The cloud, she claimed, had followed her and descended on her. Now she was with child and suspected of being a spy. It was rumoured that she had had knowledge of a Spaniard and that her elaborate story was a ruse to avert the charges that would surely track her and stick to her as fast as the phantom cloud.

Johannes would go to bed at night, his body trembling. His family's soothing words and advice not to heed the bizarre stories did little to assuage his fears.

The summer was not all grave news and dolour. The struggle of Holland's seven States to repel the Spaniards' claims on their territory was following an irresistible path of success, and the Vermeers, through his maternal side, would play no small part in this feat.

Their part had begun with Digna's father, Balthasar Gerrits, engineer, clockmaker, counterfeiter, art collector, and agent for the States. He had invented, as Digna never tired of relating to her son, a machine used by the Republic. The fact that its exact name was unknown added all the more to its brilliance, since its effect had been so subtle through the decades that its importance could not be ascribed definitely to one particular use. But Balthasar Gerrits had passed on his talent to his son, Balthens, Johannes' uncle, now an engineer in the Pioneers, the States' engineering corps, and he had worked his way up from being a humble workmaster on military fortifications for Prince Maurits and others to his present position of lieutenant.

Throughout his earliest years, the boy had been entertained, exasperated, terrified by Digna's veiled references to her brother's contribution to the nation's survival. Veiled, because of Reynier's stricture, one which had worked against this wellmeaning father: his wife and son were spies forced to eavesdrop and decode every piece of gossip about their relative that they gleaned from the soldiers who forever passed through the inn.

Johannes' head was thus a jigsaw of mysterious terms which carried the stamp of strength, purpose, and meaningful geometry. Bulwarks, half-moons, trenches, moats—all these words floated over the bleary surface of pub talk on cushions of smoke, tantalising, rugged, yet not quite within grasp. Reynier barred common soldiers from the inn, which impeded the rumours, but to turn down a captain or lieutenant, amongst whom he numbered some friends, was neither within his power nor judicious for business.

For as long as memory had allowed, Johannes had recalled the figure of a soldier sitting somewhere in either of the two inns. Sometimes, the figure would take on a concrete form and the face would be recognisable for a short time. Then it would give way to another's features. But what remained was the dominant image of an elegantly dressed man invariably turned away, the primary colours of the hat and jacket massing as if in a part of vision not yet fully explored and understood.

Then, in the form of that recurring motif, came a messagebearer for Reynier that for once he could not ignore. Captain Tobias Bres was well known to Reynier, though Johannes could not remember seeing him before this summer. He sat as they all sat, in his great red jacket embraced by a black sash, and entertained man and woman alike with stories of marvels beyond all guessing. Johannes, never a slouch, brought the workmaster his beers even more eagerly than usual. But soon it was clear there was no one else to serve because the whole inn was gathered around the handsome man.

The dark moustache dipped into the head of beer and surfaced shyly as a natural pause was registered. Bres spoke equally of two gargantuan efforts. On the Prince's orders, Bres' friends and fellow workmasters, Balthens and Van Neercassel, had built galleries over two bridges spanning the canal protecting the fort at Sas van Gent. This would protect the attacking troops as they approached the ramparts.

'But,' Bres continued, 'before they were yet done, a flood in the night destroyed their work.'

A heavy sigh escaped from mouths till now gaping in silent, mimed disbelief.

'Then the Prince went before those disheartened men and inspected the damage from the dangerous vantage of the water itself. Looking up at girders skewered in the water and the mocking, piercing sun, he discussed the situation with Balthens and Van Neercassel. The damage was made good within four days.'

This was followed by another sigh, this time of relief.

'Only then to be wrought apart by a shot from the fort. This,' he paused, perhaps expecting another sigh of frustration, though it did not come, 'was marvellously repaired after four days and the place was surrendered. Holland's fortune, for fortune always plays a part, was abetted in no small part by our friend Balthens' ingenuity.'

For once Reynier was silent on the subject of Digna's family. He looked at his son, who was now competing with a clutch of young women for the soldier's attention.

'Tell us more about Uncle Balthens,' Johannes said as his father hovered over him.

The soldier, apparently in no way unduly distracted by the competing array of décolletage on the young women, reached slowly into his pocket, and drew out a small, white, marble ball, which shone at first creamy white and which had in it an amalgam of the scientific and the artful. Only as Bres let the heavy sphere drop gently into Johannes' hands did they all realise its significance. It was a globe of the earth, its landmasses dark patches and its barely earthly creatures of the sea sitting fanciful and upright as if they would fall off the world. Johannes almost choked with joy.

'It's from Balthens. He bade me give it to you.'

'Tha . . . thank you,' Johannes stumbled out the words, now aware of Reynier's hand resting on him. Reynier patted his son on the head, sent him off running to Digna, and slipped in opposite Bres. It was not often that he could be seen sat down in conversation in his own inn.

By the end of the summer Johannes had paid his first visit to the house of Leonaert Bramer, his master for the next year. What remained from that time? Not the gentle-mannered, soft-voiced master's manners, nor the brown-gold tint of a learning the painter himself had not the heart to deride. Despite Bramer's eminence in the town, Johannes could not suppress the image of a master steeped in the weighty shadow of a school whose influence he would rather have shaken off, and his stoop seemed the direct issue of that. Light did not exist in his home or even in his palette. An older Johannes would one day be appalled at this shunning of light.

No, what was remembered above all was the first day, and its double offering. Johannes had set out that day burdened by the changed expectations of his parents. Some weeks before, he had been given a Bible and told to study it intensively in preparation. In this not even Gertruy had been able to help; she could not read Latin.

The light that day was clearer than if it had been filtered, magnified and in the process cleansed, so that most objects around him slipped to the edges of his vision, pushing him into its centre. Was the keenness of such light a mocking preparation? Leonaert Bramer's home did not strike him as the house of a painter, but rather that of a well-travelled, urbane collector. Its dimensions approached those of a patrician's residence. Led by a maid along the front hall, he observed sombre night scenes and bright still lifes; in the front room a large biblical scene took up most of one wall. The pervading tone was an ochrous brown. There seemed no escape from this, particularly within the pictures. For some time he stood transfixed in front of the virginal fascinated by subtle vertical strips of shadow on the wall below the keyboard and where this was reinforced at each end by thin, incongruent triangles. Then the door opened and the little light that came from the windows found and climbed tentatively up the body of the young woman whom he had least expected to see at such close quarters, Catharina Bolnes. Though not of the finest quality, her silver dress and lemon-hued jacket announced that she was already a woman; her hair was blonder than before, its glint sustaining itself even in this room. The fineness of her red ribbons and a pearl necklace seemed to underscore the element of precocity in this vision.

    He could not speak. She looked concerned, pivoting uneasily on one foot. Only Bramer's tardy entry saved the situation.

    'Ah, Catharina. I must apologise. Master Vermeer is my new student.'

    She remained staring at the painter as if he had insulted her and to look back at the apprentice would be the final debasement. Johannes was rescued from this mute agony sooner than he had expected. Catharina turned. The action was smooth and elegant and ended in her eyes falling slantwise across him, before resting at a point on the floor impossible to determine. But for one moment these eyes had engaged with his.

    Whether Bramer had noticed anything was doubtful, and

if he had, he could not have deciphered it, for it was only as she walked away towards the virginal after bowing, that this interchange of glances truly registered with the youth.

As they proceeded up the stairs to the studio, Johannes all the while trapped in a hallucinatory bubble from which colours, however dark, seemed sharpened and piercingly precise and their steps plotted by the next note on the meandering virginal, Bramer mumbled, 'A wonderful creature. I allow her to practise here once a week. She is from a notable family.' His words tailed off, as if he were suddenly questioning the need for such explication to a young man of Johannes' age. 'I am afraid that today I have rather overbooked myself, as you shall see.'

Before they entered the studio, Johannes sensed a displacement of air from within, followed by the rustle of heavy fabric. At first he thought his senses fooled, as the attention of the figure sitting at the table remained completely taken up by the globe to his right, as if this person were seeing such an object for the first time. Even as master and pupil entered the room, the figure remained oblivious, absorbed by the fabulous snakes and dragons of the wonderful sphere.

'Ah, Master van Rijn, I had thought you gone.'

'I still marvel at your collection, every time,' the man addressed as Van Rijn finally said. 'My apologies, I wanted to spend a moment longer.'

'It is my pleasure, Mijn Heer,' Bramer said, pleasantly taken aback. At this, before he could introduce Johannes to the man, the latter took his leave. Bramer said nothing for a while as Johannes approached the table with its outspread books of the latest knowledge and sciences, the astrolabe, and, above all, the celestial globe, in whose creamy, varnished elaboration he, too, was lost for some time. Unconsciously, the boy's fingers had started out in front of him to caress its surface. Bramer, whose instinct would normally have been to launch a strong reprimand, allowed him to continue.

Only after some time of minute survey did Johannes become aware of Bramer shifting an easel in the corner and readying a space for the lesson to begin. The bubble, which had held him in suspension for, it seemed, hours, was abruptly burst, and he was sitting with the master in front of a clean sheet of paper.

'Take note of the Scriptures,' Bramer said that same evening at supper. 'And of the gods. Too little attention is paid here, if we exclude Rembrandt, to what they have to offer, but you will profit from it.'

Bramer's advice was lost in the guttering flame of the single candle between them; the youth could not visualise Catharina as Bathsheba.

'In Italy,' Bramer continued, 'you'll find all you need.'

'And here?' Johannes asked in total innocence.

Bramer looked taken aback, as if the boy had uttered a blasphemy, but after a pause he went on to tell him of Italy. He spoke of Feti, of a fine portrait by him of a geographer resting on a globe, of his various biblical scenes, of the teeming crush of crowds in the streets and thoughts in his mind that had accompanied his progress. But, perhaps more than this, he spoke of the buildings that had arrested all of this clamour when he had stopped to look at their airy tricks of perspective, how often he would be strolling through a place admiring a ceiling painting, the engineering of such a feat at such a distance, and in what conditions! These illusions, he added, were not achieved by trial and error, but by precise calculation on paper, techniques that Johannes would one day come to master as well. Johannes, surprised by a sudden understanding and admittance to something he had never yet imagined, felt dizzy with wonder. In his mind's eye he could see Bramer's description as clearly as if he were there now in Italy.

There had been one day in a church in Rome where

Bramer had been marvelling at a circle of *putti* looking down from the painted oculus in the centre of a dome. He had noticed the teasing game the artist had played by allowing, no, by achieving, the effect of having one of the cherub's feet stepping outside the rim of the oculus as if the creature were about to drop in on the unsuspecting churchgoers. For one moment he had lifted up his arms as if to catch the babe, so perfect was the description of the figure and so convincing its cheeky intention.

And what happened at this moment? A laugh, no, more an affectionate overflow from a spirit emanating as much from the walls of that place as from flesh, had edged through the slim fault in Bramer's concentration, bringing him around to face a creature of such beauty that he indeed worried that his bookish concentration on geometry had got the better of him and that he was no longer able to distinguish between a human form and a cunning mathematical projection veiled in paint. But she laughed again and looking at her he recognised a biblical scene he had already imagined before this moment. She was the perfect model, created as much from the artist's mind as based on the life.

'She was of low birth, and only a few years younger than me, mark you no great advantage for a young man of our calling, should our intentions swim in Amor's direction. Yet I am of the opinion that love can bridge the greatest chasm.'

Bramer eyed Johannes steadily. The boy shifted uneasily. It was the first time Bramer had referred to romance.

'And my model she became,' he added, truncating the story sharply, it seemed, to a disappointed Johannes.

Bramer played pensively with a fish knife for a while, moving it against the table cover, turning it over and again as if he were dabbing at his palette to build up a ridge of impasto paint, then said, 'There is a picture of mine. Come. Let me show it to you.'

Johannes followed him upstairs to a room at the back. As

they went along the barely lit corridor, Johannes tried to decipher the small paintings they passed, but was able to establish little besides the country of origin of most of these—Italy. Now, more than ever, he felt his lack of knowledge, knowledge of the Bible, and the lack of an apparatus to interpret these constructions.

In the room there were rows of canvases and panels, leaning against the wall, some covered over. As Bramer searched around, Johannes tried to ignore the pronounced gastric pop he heard on a few occasions. Bramer was muttering something, eliding this occasionally with a whimper as he searched around— Johannes accompanying him gingerly all the while, attempting to direct the light of a candle so as to illuminate but not damage.

Then there was a small cry of recognition as Bramer found what he was looking for. Johannes held back various paintings while Bramer lifted up the large panel and took it over to a table by the window. It showed a scene that at last the young man knew: the Magdalene washing the feet of Christ.

The Christ figure sat in a dull purple shift, while Mary, in blue and gold, laved his feet, cupping them as if she could foresee the imprimatur of wounds yet to come. About them stood the Pharisees, looking on with disbelief at the ministering sinner, yet the gesturing and posture of each figure and a suffusive yellow tint united the whole group.

Johannes recognised the mastery of technique here, though this alone would not have been enough to hold his interest. That element came from the Magdalene herself; she was indescribably beautiful, much too beautiful for the dignity of the picture, with her full strawberry cheeks, a charmingly duck-like expression, and dark gabled eyebrows. Had Bramer indeed ever shown this work to anyone before now, a work that suffocated under a layer of dust that Johannes could now smell burning in the corona of the candle's flame?

'She is the one,' Bramer said, and some time passed

before Johannes connected these words with those about the woman in the church that Bramer had told him of downstairs.

He wanted to ask more. What had happened to her? Had she been in other paintings? But he could not. For now he could only receive messages and impressions like an empty canvas.

'She will come again,' said Bramer.

But now Johannes was not so certain. Who did his master mean? When he finally left that night, the words still dominated his thoughts: *She will come again.* Along the darkened streets, which seemed to take their shading from the very surroundings of Bramer's house and his night scenes, his mind was an abacus of calculations; he should see Catharina once a week if fate would allow such a pleasing arrangement, for surely Bramer had been referring to her? And if not once a week, then there would be a mean number to rely on, for . . . how long would it be?

He had no words for the sensations that visited him in the following nights, just as there had been no precedents for what sights had called them into being. Only that night, when he had heard the woman and the sailor in the darkened tunnel and glimpsed her semi-nakedness, had the door begun to open. Yet in shame he had slammed that door shut. Why? He did not know where the shame came from. It lay not in any censorious attentions of Digna's or Reynier's, nor of his teachers.

He tried to distract himself by thinking of Tanneken, the maid. The picture she usually presented was that of a sturdy woman involved in layer upon layer of chores from plucking chicken to bringing the tiles to a spectral sheen. However, one day, he had returned home from Van Aelst's studio earlier than usual. The rooms at the back of the inn seemed as if becalmed. There was neither Tanneken's customary scuttling about, nor was any window open. Johannes could not even hear any sounds from the inn. Only one sound seemed to exist and this was ill defined, a kind of murmur with intermittent pauses. After checking the ground-floor rooms, he moved on upstairs and passed down the corridor.

He was close to satisfying his curiosity. The door to Tanneken's room was open, and her flat bulk was massed in shadow in the near corner. Yet the shadow itself confused him; the form rocked occasionally—perhaps she was crying? Then contact with a loose floorboard produced a creak, and this in turn a startled movement of the shadow. He had no choice but to identify himself.

'Tanneken?'

There was no reply, only the movement and a hasty rustling of fabric.

'Tanneken?'

Then an undeniable sound, the cry of a baby, and, as he entered the room, the sight he would not forget for a long time. The baby's mouth was moving through space to an object neither the child was truly aware of, nor which Johannes himself had totally been conscious of till now. Out of a network of undone lace on her bodice the conical perfection of a milk-tipped breast sloped down to the tiny mouth, the focus of the woman's gaze, itself absorbed in the baby's own absorption. It seemed that this configuration might last indefinitely. The baby was content in milky oblivion whilst the intertwined reticulation of lace and this soft purposeful flesh competed for Johannes' attention. When she finally looked up, it was not in reprimand, but by way of explanation, for it was not Tanneken, but a woman much like her in appearance, except a little younger.

'Oh, I'm Elizabeth, Tanneken's sister. You must be young Johannes?'

'Yes,' he said, relieved that she was not angry.

'This is Maertge. It's a pretty name, don't you think?'

She held Maertge up again so that he could get a full view.

The memory of that strange encounter diverted him for some time—he never mentioned the episode to Tanneken, nor she to him—yet something in it was cognate with what he had thought to escape and thus it only succeeded in bringing on further thoughts of Catharina. The shame rose in him as she flickered across the screen of his mind, as his body contorted itself to the measure of his visions, and then his seed was out, seeping down into the linen just as he was descending to a lower level of sweet unconsciousness.

That seeping loss stayed with the apprentice for the rest of his time with Van Aelst, a constant reprimand and badge of guilt, as if it were the very reason for his misfortune in not seeing Catharina again, for indeed, he was not to see her again at Bramer's. The 'once a week', on which his thoughts had dwelt so much, became a pocket in time which existed only when he was absent, as if time itself had been recalibrated to exclude a fortuitous meeting. To add to this, the bars of any virginal or clavecin he overheard became a rack for his anticipatory thoughts.

Such thoughts were eventually subsumed by another romance that had taken him unawares: a hunger for knowledge, which could only be fed and partly sated by his present master, though a truer designation might have been flirtation. Flirtation, because there was an uncertainty that derived from the fact that Johannes knew, intuitively, many of the things he was taught, yet he had to force himself to understand those calculations from the Italians, those marriages of unlikely pigments, their chemical compositions. In fact he could only deceive himself into believing he understood because his brain was slow and he had no ideas.

If, for example, he successfully multiplied two figures in his head, even when he had been complimented by his teacher, he would find himself going back to confirm the result, again and again; only then could he find some peace. Or, it took the example of a child's toy, a cup with a ball attached to it by a length of string, to explain how the tilt of the earth and its constant rotation determined the gradual slipping from one season into another around the world as the months passed. And it was only when Bramer produced a charming diagram, in which the sun and the planets seemed to move around each other in an other-worldly dance, that Johannes started to feel that certain facts about the cosmos would not be beyond his grasp.

A harsher man than Bramer would have confided his doubts to Reynier, telling him of his son's mathematical struggles, but Bramer held his peace; and meanwhile, the gap of despair that Johannes had started to feel was slowly giving way to an unexpected, tentative awakening in the boy.

The painter had again invited Johannes to dine with him. The place was unusually light, the spring's promise buttressed by an array of candles that stood sentinel before canvases Johannes had barely noticed till now. It was a very different scene to that initiatory, fleeting tour during that first invitation. Before they would eat, Johannes would see all these works, guided by Bramer's whispered commentary. What they saw, the artists' names, their towns of origin, their subjects, meant in themselves little to the apprentice except in one common regard; none of these painters was from Delft. To be sure, the generally muted colours of the Utrecht artists along with their themes of music and revelry attracted him, while the historical and classical scenes of The Hague and Haarlem seemed to ground him where before only uncertainty and abstraction had reigned. This impression was reinforced by the occasional Italian scene that Bramer had no doubt brought back with him. And there were other, everyday scenes, captured in a curious manner, which sometimes startled him, sometimes left him ambivalent.

Bramer had led him past these, as if at once mourning an invisible loss and drawing a curtain over them. When they finally sat down to eat, the master's words fitted over the boy's thoughts and he knew that Bramer's fleeting observations had become like honey slowly accreting in the cells of a comb, or like a waxy grid which had slowly infused his brain—a matrix that would suffuse his mind for many years.

'Delft is not a place for you, young Johannes, not for now. The place is dying, it is insipid. I myself have played a worthy part, but I have seen better.' In the encroaching dusk the streaks of brown in the irises of his grey eyes seemed to stretch away like rivers running off a globe.

Johannes felt the return of a sense of loss, of that feeling of displacement he had experienced in the inn when he had run away, only to be tracked down by his father. He had come to appreciate and rely on Bramer's gentle observations, and now he faced that loss more concretely than ever before.

'Your father,' Bramer said eventually, 'wills that you go to Amsterdam. This decision he has taken on my advice; he sees that you should go into the world. For he sees as keenly as I do that you are in danger of retreating from your talents, however slow they are to show themselves.'

At this, he coughed, drawing his hand across his mouth as dextrously as if he were applying a technique he wished to keep secret from another artist.

'Besides,' he went on, 'he was apprenticed there, and he has friends who will lodge you. You will see more of the Italians, more of architecture, more practising artists, more, indeed, of everything.'

Johannes was not excited by the idea of Amsterdam, nor was he in awe. His first thoughts were of whether he would ever see Catharina again, yet this anxiety was soothed by Bramer's concluding words.

'We shall remain friends, Johannes. And when you return you will be master not only of paint, but of the world.' Whereupon, he winked at the boy, and led him along the dark corridors to the front door.

\* \* \*

## The Dance of Geometry

Several weeks before his departure Johannes wandered one day into the Nieuwe Kerk, on the Great Market Square. Here he had been baptised, but the family's visits had been few and mainly on national occasions. In years to come he would long debate with himself if anything would have been different had he entered on any other day, at any other hour, when the light would not have allowed such a particular view.

Outside, the clouds had aligned themselves to create a strange rhythm of chevroned light leading to the church. The marketers were oblivious, and indeed the square was almost empty. Inside, narrow ferruginous sheets of light were thrust into the aisle and intercepted the nave in a storm of chrome violence belied by the surrounding quiet. It was not this vision that fascinated the boy, but the sudden access of the view down the nave, then back up again to the ambulatory before which a vertiginous competition of receding, approaching, converging and clashing lines pressed up against him and drew him in at the same time. And the vehicle for this effect, the black and white tiles and white colonnaded pillars, was for a few seconds wondrously invisible to him. He recalled days of hard work with Bramer, when the master had striven to drive home the rules of perspective.

It had been his first afternoon in such instruction. Bramer had taken out various folios, many of them valuable, to show him a series of drawings which, in the Italian manner, posited a single eye-point and the place where each ray of light intersected a plane, and the methods by which any given point within the frame was brought forward on that plane. One method involved plan and elevation and the plotting of all these points on one master sheet. In another method, the whole construction was anchored in the realistic representation of a grid of floor tiles; this became the measure and foundation for all subsequent additions of objects and all other things seen. The mathematics intrigued and frightened him at the same time, yet it was this that gave the whole a purpose, that drew him on and in, that acted as the structure that came before what was seen, its guiding lines the peel that could be stretched back to reveal the inner fruit of space.

Yet there was frustration in this example. In Johannes' version, executed in pen, certain lines would not meet as they should. Extrapolated, they would proceed out of the bounds allotted to them, and planes twisted into asymmetrical contortions he had never seen before. The thing was impossible to determine successfully. Bramer, passing by in a heavily embroidered coat, seeing this geometric monster, seemed on the point of saying something, but went on all the same.

Now, standing in this church, Johannes felt light and disembodied, as if his eyes and mind, floating up and surveying everything, were taking in three different points of convergence, to the left, right and in the distance.

He paid his respects, and walked towards the entrance, passing and nodding at the artist Emanuel de Witte, some sixteen years his elder, whom he had occasionally seen calling upon Van Aelst. De Witte, his moustache turned up in the customary elaboration, was an artist whose work Johannes as yet had little occasion to admire. Inexplicably, Johannes turned and watched the artist walk into the church and consider the same area of space that had so recently impressed him. But De Witte, he knew, was not a church painter. When the older artist abruptly turned, Johannes deferentially continued on.

The pupils of his father's eyes shifted almost imperceptibly, as if attempting to lose themselves in the white globules of reflection that rode their edges. This, and a certain awkward, turned-inwardness, lent him a look that Johannes found furtive and unsettling. Reynier and his son remained leaning against the side of the barge. The sun was behind them, settling like red ochre dust on roofs and patches of shore. The figures that they left behind them seemed disproportionately small now, as if aware that they were being disowned.

Johannes wondered whether his father was ashamed of something to come, or overly conscious of having left Digna and Gertruy to manage on their own for the next four days.

'I have in any case business to settle, paintings to buy,' was what he had said to Digna, who had shown little resistance. Some of Reynier's strange mood was at least explained when Johannes saw him put his hand into the pocket of his new coat, carefully drawing out a long-stemmed ivory pipe, and begin to fill it with tobacco. Johannes' eyes widened. He had never seen him smoke before.

'Not a word,' said Reynier, winking.

They were alone on the barge, the bargeman lost in the language he shared with the Amsterdam-bound horse. The town was now a stretched rhomboid of amber in the near distance, a huge tent with the Nieuwe Kerk as its central supporting pole, yet Johannes could still not turn himself away. Indeed, there was a kermis today, and his thoughts were concentrated on his absence from the carnival that was to take place there, for Catharina would surely be present.

Johannes slept for some hours, waking to find his father's heavy coat and a much-altered grey-blue carapace of sky weighing down on them. Reynier had succeeded in engaging the truculent bargeman in conversation. They were in fact laughing. They had discovered a point of contact in their personal histories; they had both worked in Amsterdam in their younger days as caffa workers. Johannes thought he caught, in the blur of his father's fragmented, nostalgic reminiscences, a sense of regret, of lost opportunities. Could that really be possible?

'But it was not then what it is now,' was the most concrete expression he heard, this from the bargeman. To the best of Johannes' knowledge, Reynier had not returned to Amsterdam more than three or four times since his birth.

They sat on deck for most of the day, eating Gouda, which

the bargeman gently portioned off with a knife. Constantly, the boy found his eye falling on the man's enormous, roughly lined hand. Reynier, for his part, seemed almost transfixed by the blade. Father and son were bound in unstated mutual reminiscences where other knife blades had glinted, memories of another kind now, barely aware that huge church spires and windmills, under a crowding, empty sky, were slipping slowly by, dwarfed by aloof cattle whipping the air nonchalantly with their tails.

Towards evening Johannes drifted off again into a sleep whose rhythm was defined by the barge's motion. When he finally awoke, it was to find the city had come stealthily upon him, engulfing him. He had not been accorded a secret entry: his would not be an outsider's view. He was already there, inside.

With that approach to the city, that narrowing of the horizon, the buildings that stretched themselves upwards to stand to attention in rows like a dignified burgher family inspecting their mirrored reflections before posing for a portrait, came a pragmatic, distanced father. Never prolix, Reynier now set about the various alleys and side-streets to search out inns and illustrious residences alike in which to talk of and deal in art in a functional fashion, tailoring his speech to suit the class of dealer. During this time Johannes remained in suspense about his first Amsterdam master. Was the knowledge being withheld out of shame, he wondered? For all his father's praise of his own son's talents, Johannes knew it would not be Rembrandt van Rijn. They could not have afforded that.

Johannes sensed in his father the imminence of an announcement.

Before they entered the building, Reynier stood looking up at the façade, as if in some private calculation.

'What is it, father?'

'The street lies east west, so the studio should be north-facing. That is a good sign,' he replied, and squeezed his son's hand.

Johannes feigned recognition. He could never orient himself instantly. He knew *how*; the task was simple enough, but the deduction arrived as if it had first passed through many hands along many corridors and antechambers. They passed into the darkened hall and were about to proceed up the staircase, which they found midway down. Reynier had momentarily disengaged his hand and was walking slightly ahead. Out of anxiety? Pride? What was the hurry? In Johannes' mind, the questions overlayered each other. Was this, then, the manner in which he was finally to be separated? Delft, Mechelen, Digna, Gertruy . . . Catharina.

They were still striding up the stairs when a rush of sound from behind, like an unidentified nocturnal animal, buffeted them slightly. An expanding vertical rectangle of purplish-red activity, two forms stumbling, the raucous voice of a woman in the background, the sudden narrowing of the rectangle of the door closing to a dark, penumbral sliver.

'What? What?' slurred one. 'At this time?' Then, seemingly coming to his senses, he slapped the other, handsomer man on the back in an effort to propel him towards the street. 'We shall speak, Gerard. Off with you.'

Yet before the young man named Gerard could move down the corridor, Johannes caught a gleam in his eye, which made him stand rigid. He could not fathom the source of such an intense reflection out of such darkness. Years later he would be able to recall the young man's bearing, his dandyish stance, the studied flamboyance of his dress, his moustache, and, above all, a gaze which fixed him and knew him—as if it would cast an image of him instantly, create an exterior mould around him for all to see, and define his being—even as it seemed to slide away, searching for something peripheral. The sudden intrusion of the inn along with the brusque introduction of this unlikely pair into this closed-off passageway—the co-mingling of acid beer breath and a young man's perfume—riveted Johannes. Then, as the remaining man went about lighting the corridor and they continued to stand there, the face of his first Amsterdam master slowly flickered into view. It was a sharp, enquiring one.

'Fox, you old . . .' were Van Loo's first words, curtailed promptly though not irascibly by Reynier's insistence on the new name of Vermeer. Rather than allow them to proceed upstairs, Van Loo ushered them into the inn.

Having succeeded in distancing his son from Mechelen, Reynier might have been disappointed by the propinquity of the inn to Van Loo's academy, but if so he did not show it. In fact, at one point as they drank, he attempted to make light of this concern, saying to his son, 'Being so close to an inn may not please your mother, but such a place is a fact of life, is it not?' Then he winked.

Van Loo, a stern presence in dress and manner even in these circumstances, struck Johannes as cold, academic, as if the knowledge he had was a barrier. He had a fragile frame, which was hidden beneath neat, subdued clothes. His face was pale, as if powdered. His small, wide-open turquoise eyes, bordered by short spidery lashes, were the only point of interest and even this seemed to stem from their attempt to avoid contact. To Johannes, he seemed both constantly looking and not looking; looking when the boy's gaze was elsewhere, eyes averted when an attempt was made to engage. It did not bode well.

'The times are good now,' he began. 'I have my ambitions, yet my life-blood is the studio. I have my apprentices and I have the boys who come to the academy once or twice a week.'

He paused a moment, fixing Reynier for a second, only

to allow his eyes to continue quickly on their fugitive course. 'I am no longer cheap, Reynier.'

Reynier shrugged, as if to say he would be able to meet any sum, canting his head slightly towards Johannes, perhaps seeking conferral. 'How much?'

'One hundred.'

Reynier let out a slow sigh. 'I did not expect less.'

'I can find occasional work outside for the boy, and it includes board and lodging, if you so wish.'

'That would be good, Johannes, to be so close to your study?'

'Yes, Father, yes.' He was excited at the prospect before him, but conscious too of wanting to please his father, even though this would confirm the distance that must now grow between them.

Van Loo still did not look at Johannes. 'I have more and more contacts. That Gerard,' he said wistfully, as if lamenting the absence of a mistress. 'He has a rare talent. Such delicacy.'

But beyond this mention of the young man that they had seen in the corridor, Van Loo did not explain himself further.

'I instruct in the essential: mythical, biblical, historical. I do not undertake to do any more than provide a grounding in these accepted fields. And technique, of course . . .'

'It is understood,' Reynier confirmed. Johannes, so astounded to see that for once his father showed no inclination to argue the terms, barely heard his father's next words, 'You can lodge him tonight?'

'Then it is done,' said Van Loo, whereupon they shook hands.

Johannes did not see much of his new lodgings till the morning; Van Loo did not bother to light more than two candles in the academy after they had staggered out of the inn. Before going up, they had stood awhile in the street, watching Johannes' father become steadily absorbed by the shadows of a nearby canal bridge.

In his room that night Johannes thought he saw a slight, feminine, candle-bearing figure, but he was too drowsy from drink to be certain. The fleeting image took on more substance in the night when he thought he heard the sounds of revelling above, particularly the voice of a young woman, but by the morning he could not say if he had dreamt this aural counterpart. When he finally awoke, it was to the determinedly real sound of feet padding about and furniture being scraped around upstairs. His room, he deduced from the position of the sun, must be directly above the studio.

He came out of the room and was pushed aside abruptly by three boys slightly younger than himself rushing up the last flight of stairs, one devouring the last portion of a wedge of bread, another clutching a bright green apple to his chest as if afraid it might be snatched away from him at any time. Johannes did not hurry after them but stopped to study a series of framed engravings from Van Veen's *Amorum Emblemata*. He remembered Bramer. The series ran along the corridor wall, ending at a right angle to its companions, on the door to Van Loo's studio, with a depiction of a cupid holding aloft a card displaying the numeral one, along with an exhortation to lovers to have only one partner. The muscular thighs and downcast, concentrated look of the figure left him feeling strangely alone.

A raised voice finally released him from his entrancement. It was Van Loo, bellowing at someone in the studio. As Johannes arrived, a young woman, perhaps the same person he had glimpsed the previous evening with the candle, was once more slipping out of view and the three boys were scrabbling for places in front of their easels. Another four boys already sat working at theirs. On a small raised platform a model sat depicting Diana, whom he identified from a makeshift crown with a sickle moon.

The doubly muted light of mid-morning shone through

the oiled paper of the blind of one window. Johannes became conscious of the woman's beauty, yet feared eye contact. He wanted to hide away, to grind colours, or better, retreat into the adjacent room into which the elusive figure had flitted. Through the open door of that room he saw the edge of a canvas suspended lightly by tacking stitches within a frame, but from where Johannes sat, no image could be deciphered.

His anonymity was not to last. In front of all his pupils, and to the utter surprise of Johannes, Van Loo called everyone to attention to listen to a paean directed at none other than the new boy.

'Quiet now,' Van Loo began. 'This is young Johannes Vermeer, a boy of much promise,' and here the teacher's eyes searched his captive audience accusingly, 'from the city of Delft. We might learn much from our fellow Hollanders. He is to be treated well, you hear.'

The mumbling of one of the boys was followed by a few sniggers, and mostly cursory glances, while an arch smile floated over the model's face. The rumbling of a young stomach heightened, then punctured, the momentary amusement.

The morning passed with Van Loo circling the boys and delivering assessments of their efforts. In between, he would pick up a volume of Ovid's *Metamorphoses* and read episodes relating to the subject of their drawing. He said little of Johannes' work but noticed his occasional, nervous turning around towards the interior studio, which he thought must be where Van Loo worked on commissioned paintings.

And it was true. While a dutiful Johannes set about depicting the goddess, little inspired by the violent narrative, another Johannes attempted to fill in the details of the empty canvas in the room behind him. When Van Loo passed by him and looked at his efforts, he did not say anything, but to the others he praised or reprimanded or advised. The day was passed entirely within the studio, with Johannes sketching—in addition to a model—a cream-white plaster putto, suspended from the ceiling and lowered by a pulley, and a skull, placed accusingly on a small table in front of him.

When the others had been sent home, he was invited to dine with Van Loo. The meal had passed in almost complete silence. He surveyed the crisp, frozen eyes and fleshless bones of the fish on his plate, the still glistening slice of lemon to its side; the apprentice had not had the courage to disperse its contents, so uncertain was he of Amsterdam etiquette. From this, Johannes' attention turned to watch a final distended diamond of light edge across the wall behind his master's back. He was curious; it was perhaps the only pure, unfiltered light he had seen that first day and yet the source of its shimmering amber sunburst could not be located.

Uncertain of himself, bewildered by Van Loo's sudden taciturnity, he yearned for the day to end, for a secret to be yielded up. When Van Loo finally spoke, his words disappointed his pupil.

'Do I perceive in you, young Johannes, a lack of patience?'

The question hovered like bittersweet smoke in the air, detached from the issuer, as if Van Loo would have denied responsibility for it if asked.

'Mijn Heer, I want to show things as they are.'
'And not as they are meant to be?'
'I want to paint light. Light cannot lie.'
'Drawing is a tedious chore to you, I presume?'
'I like paint.'
'You will learn, Johannes, that you will have to discard much of what you do to reach your goal; you will have to throw away gold to achieve even adequacy. There is no shortcut.'

Johannes said nothing.

'You talk about light as if it were your brother, or perhaps a young sweetheart that you are determined to possess. You can be too close to such a love. You must learn to approach it . . .

indirectly, just as it oftentimes illuminates what we ourselves perceive. Remember, if something is a certain colour, blue, let's say, it is so because the material of which it is made says "no" more forcefully to light than to dark. Yellow, for example, denies dark more than it admits white.'

Johannes nodded, but Van Loo asked, 'You know this?'

'Yes, Mijn Heer.'

On his way to his room, the mystery of the unidentified figure was solved as he climbed the stairs. It was the maid, who, he judged, moved as if to escape light, shielding herself from the lamp that she held. She did not look at him as they passed each other.

In the night he dreamt as he never had before. He dreamt of Gertruy, of a closeness to her which defied his nature, which made him cry in his sleep: she was lost to him. He was woken by the sound of furniture being moved around above, and the sound of a woman's laugh, accompanied by the deeper counterpoint of a man's.

Lighting a candle, he passed up the stairs to the studio. The door was open. The eyes of alabaster and marble busts reflected back the yellow of the guttering candle while the putto hovered above, both as if turning slightly from a draught, and as if he would indicate the way. The cords from the blinds seemed to situate a momentary vanishing point whose orthogonals, with their straight lines meeting in the central vanishing point of this as-yet-to-be-composed picture ran along the lower batten of a canvas pushed aside in the corner, continuing along the window sills where moonlight lay like silver satin. But a third source of light softened and made this vision possible. He turned round to Van Loo's studio and saw through a vertical rectangle part of a scene replicated by another canvas there. He stopped moving.

There, in that room, he saw a quartet of figures, two men and two women, the one woman to the left holding a violin, the standing man, a lute. Further along, another man leant towards a well-dressed woman whose chair was toppling over in her effort to restrain him and prevent him damaging the discarded bass viol at her feet; all were seated except the lute-playing man. Johannes could not have said how far the man's entreaties were welcomed by the woman, but he found himself wishing the man would stop his advances.

When the man finally did so, and turned around to pick up a wine glass, Johannes recognised the man called Gerard, and with this, in the figure of the lute player, Van Loo; in the courted woman, the model of the previous day; in the other woman, the maid. Pose or painted scene, he had been entranced to such a degree that he had stopped breathing, and realising this, he suddenly took in a gulp of air, which, when he let it out, sounded like the sigh of a sated voyeur. The figures turned, the hollow sound of the lute being placed on the table came as a shock, and Johannes retreated into the darkness from which he had come.

He read the letter, the first ever addressed directly to him, through the filtered emerald light of the main studio, as if this would shield him from what he feared.

*Dear Johannes,*

*I write with good news, but brief... I am to marry within the month. I shall be the wife of Anthony. Surely this comes as no surprise? Mother and Father are both overjoyed, father especially so. Anthony's reputation is growing and to have good, reliable frames so near to hand will aid Father in his business, which too is prospering. The banns are being published now. I shall write to say when it will be. Mother and Father send their love. They are more than busy now, but they will write soon, as should you...*

*Love, Gertruy*

The year passed without event, save for Gertruy's marriage, which was a small, modest affair, though on that day Johannes believed that, for the first time he could recall, he saw her radiant with the face of true contentment. His drawing improved little during that time. His world was once more an interior one, yet there was one event that stood out.

The scene that he had witnessed in Van Loo's studio returned, in two different configurations, its players variously recast, as if that scene had till now existed on a plane so close to his vision that he had not been able to interpret it correctly. The first manifestation of the scene was indirect, a background observation to a larger unveiling. On that day Van Loo took him up to the studio to show off *his* Diana. The older man stood, beaming, as if illumined by the pale, reflecting, brimming chest of the goddess. Her constant, steady gaze apart, who else was the captive onlooker but the viewer himself? Actaeon, who had been spying on Diana as she was undressed by her maids, was nowhere to be seen.

Johannes could at first see little to enthuse about. Diana's handmaids had been made to adopt awkward, untenable postures; even the goddess herself had one foot raised strangely on a rock, which seemed to separate that leg from the purposefulness of the rest of the body. It was, however, in the fine highlights of one of the hair bands and sleeves, the similar decorative metallic tracing around Diana's waist and in the soft gleaming undulations of the pointing maid to her right, that Johannes' attention was ultimately held. And it was during this survey that he noticed the scene of the merry company on the wall behind the Diana, the company to whose nocturnal genesis decorum would not allow Johannes to allude. It was finished, but it was evident that the faces of the participants had been altered to deny all similarity to the models he had espied that night. When he mentioned this painting, which hung on the wall to the left, neglected, with seemingly no other image to counterbalance it, Van Loo dismissed it as a minor work in a genre he was happy to be leaving behind.

Now, just as Johannes recognised this painted scene from its nocturnal incarnation, it would yet take another form, both concrete and questionable. It was to come and take him within its dark cloak, sweep him away, and return him, at once empowered and bereft.

The invitation—or had it been a summons?—had reached Johannes, stealthily, via the hands of Van Loo. The master must have known the contents of the message, as he had sent the maid, whose name was Annetje, almost immediately to Johannes' room to help him dress, along with a new black cape.

'The master says you are to wear this,' she said, offering him the cape that had been held in the hand that had carried the lantern.

When she said this, he was still at the window scanning the creamy paper, its colour yellowed by a hurried dusk, which had left clusters of dogs barking as if at some amorphous evil power.

'But before that, there's a little matter of a wash.'

Johannes stared at her.

'A wash?'

'Yes, your hair. The master said it should be done in the style.'

That mass of loose lank hair was now immersed in water several times and the scalp mercilessly massaged by hands he had always presumed soft but which were in fact crumbly-hard, like the charcoal he used for drawing. During the operation he felt her small bosom press insistently against his shoulder. He blushed. Yet there was nothing indecent about this woman. Had she really taken part in that night vision?

He emerged from the whole process with curls, cape, and hat—a young gentleman about town. After a brief inspection by Van Loo, who said little of consequence but beamed with a palpable pride, he was presented to the streets.

Johannes had seen so little of the town till now. His image of the place had been restricted to those few locales he had had to go to—Loeman the affable supplier of pigments, Cornelisz., the frame maker, the occasional tavern, the Dam. He had kept away from the harbour, assiduously, rarely admitting his fear, often expecting that woman, by turns impudent, whorish, weeping, abused, and the craggy sailor to reach out at him from the shadow of another arch. Now, where was he going? It seemed, in the direction of just such a consecution of shadows and arches as he dreaded, down the Oudezijdsachterburgwal towards the docks.

Yet what of Gerard? He surely did not live here? *That Gerard.* Van Loo's emphasis wound along a spiralling chamber in his head. What had his teacher meant?

Looking around now, he was not certain where he was. His contemplation, or perhaps that narrow tunnel of intention he was moving through, had diverted him so that he found himself once more looking at that prematurely ravaged face of the harlot from the Delft docks of his childhood. Was it indeed she? He was standing by a doorway where a crowd was jeering abuse at the pilloried woman. Her face, her face, a syphilitic rubric blossoming on a mackerel metal ground, her décolletage hideously proffering what could not be partaken of. He wanted to cover it over; he could not, could only shiver, fixing the crowd balefully, disembodied as he was, because they were the true objects of his study. They were the observers observed.

The hand, when it came, was stealthy in its arrival, but welcome in its purchase nevertheless. Johannes found himself staring into the jet-black eyes of Gerard.

'Johannes, where are you going?' he said, and took the boy's arm, like a lover.

He had overshot Gerard's residence, a tavern, by a few

doors. The place was like the tavern below Van Loo's academy, only a little more gentile, the faces more varied, the clientèle more mercantile than marine or military, the serving girls more decorative and conscious of their manners.

Gerard looked on at the scene as if slightly embarrassed. He led Johannes over to a table where a soldier sat. Like Gerard, he too wore a moustache, and was handsome. His clothes, though well lived in, were the source of some pride: his dun leather jerkin, his plumed helmet, his sash. Yes, again the sash. Johannes would like to have handled it, but propriety and dignity held him back.

The soldier was bewailing the truce with Spain and the waning of hostilities with England. 'I shall be demoted to carrying out lowly tasks like bearing messages,' he moaned. 'Invariably unwelcome.'

Gerard eyed him archly, then said, 'And wenching.'

'There is no satisfaction in that.'

'Perhaps you would profit from some variety.'

'What? The pox, syphilis, or crabs?'

Gerard smiled, but as one who is reluctant to concede a point. 'There is more than one way to sleep with a whore.'

The soldier looked suddenly concerned, his features engaged, as if to accede to a familiar but distasteful expression. 'Really, should we be speaking like this in front of the boy?'

Gerard, who had guided Johannes in and locked him in the narrow space between him and the wall, put his arm around the young man and clutched him in avuncular fashion. Johannes was doubly surprised, both by the manoeuvre and by the coolness of Gerard's flesh, and he swam in a momentary panic, unable to place the seat of his fear, which resembled the great emptiness he had felt on the night of his flight from the stevedore and the whore. Yet he was captivated by the soldier, by the sight of the occasional elegant woman who passed by, by the intoxicating richness of clothing worn by many of the customers, man and woman alike.

The soldier, now courted by the whore, moved away from them, and Gerard, perhaps aware of Johannes' discomfort, moved around to the other side. The two studied each other, Johannes' eyes occasionally wandering in a search for some meaning or reassurance. These elegant men and women, card-players, whores, the occasional soldier, merchants, the innkeeper's dogs, the straw-filled buckets under the tables into which the women occasionally emptied their tankards, the smoke which burnt his eyes, the radiating foot-warmers: should they say something to him? Each coaxed in him a consuming compassionate interest, yet together they knitted a worrying, cloying skein of which he wanted to be rid.

His attention shifted to Gerard's eyes, which were engaged in their own perusal, those orbits that seemed to carry darkness within them as if to confer it on the unwary. How could he be open to taking in a view of things when his own gaze threatened to impose an a priori image on whatever he saw?

'Do not judge too hastily,' Gerard spoke at last. Johannes tried to pretend he did not understand Gerard's unexpected words, words that seemed to read and comment on Johannes' own view of the older man. But he knew they were a mild rebuke for what must be clear to an intelligent observer; Johannes was uncomfortable here, not out of fear, but out of disapproval.

Johannes sensed that they were waiting for something, some appearance, that the real matter at hand would be kept at bay until that time. That it would take the form of a woman was no revelation, though which woman, mediated by the dress, colour, and texture assigned to her, that would constitute the surprise. Shortly after the woman whom Johannes had noticed had passed by them, Gerard stood up, saying nothing, and went upstairs to a room whose door was just visible at the end of the landing. He had left Johannes with another tankard to occupy him for the time. The soldier, too, had disappeared. The waitress had ruffled his hair in a friendly gesture, from which he had shrunk back, feeling himself the object of the whole inn's attention. But he could not leave without telling Gerard.

To extended ribald commentary he climbed the stairs towards the room to which Gerard had retired. The sound of a lute, offset by small sallies of laughter, was dimly audible as he stood outside. He knocked, and the laughter stopped, then continued. Another knock drew the same sequence of reactions. He opened the door gently. The familiarity of the scene, even partly screened and framed as it was by a wall hanging, pulled him, strangely, vertiginously, in. And perhaps it was all the more disconcerting as the participants showed no sign of surprise or outrage; rather, Gerard, even as he and the girl fell and swayed in the darkness of their intimate carousing and music making, seemed to beckon him. The soldier from downstairs and another woman passed before him and disappeared as if rubbed out with a cloth on a canvas.

*What do they want of me? Oh, let me go, now. I want to go back!*

Gerard stood up, adjusting his breeches slightly. He seemed to take in a breath as if to cancel out incipient indignation. For the first time Johannes became aware of the artist's height and stature. His magnetism was startling.

*I want to be like you, but I never shall,* said the slightly plump, wide-jawed Johannes, but the words did not issue from his lips.

Gerard let go of the girl's hand and glided towards Johannes, his hand coming to rest on the boy's shoulder heavily, like that of a workman. He lifted Johannes' chin, almost as if to allow the boy to study those delicate, effeminate cilia of his. Could Gerard feel his trembling?

'Boy, do not be afraid. You will thank me, later.'

Johannes stared, pleadingly. Did Gerard really mean what he, Johannes, thought?

'Think carefully and see attentively. This is your subject, and of it too you are the subject.'

And his subject was undeniable. As he approached her, he saw that her face did not contain that perceived harshness that his mind had painted from a penumbral, recessed distance. She was smiling, he thought. He could not be absolutely certain of this; it might have been the play of the nearby guttering candle on her second, powdered skin. It seemed to him that this was in fact a face that did not trust itself to smile, should the true face ever be revealed.

Now, another Johannes looked onto this scene as if a witness to his own actions. This Johannes stood back a few footsteps into the room, while the other, enticed by the parallel receding lines of the canopy bed, walked on. She, framed by a triangle of dark beyond the partly opened hanging of the canopy, let fall a stocking nonchalantly to the floor. Doubly framed as she was by the first, screening curtain and then by the canopy's, she seemed to centre his being, while the objects around him made her stand out as if in relief, pushing her forward to him. Yet something else drew him beyond this geometric pull, beyond the promise of her body. At this distance it was still only an intimation, another sliver of darkness, and he awoke to it as her smile awoke to him: the space between her teeth pulled him in further, adding something feral to and undermining the attempted elegance in the smile. What he felt now for the first time was not his own; it was being taken from him by a force stronger than himself. He wanted to give it, but that could not be; and what he received was not given, either. It was being taken by him.

Another thought now flitted through his mind: he had not heard Gerard leave the room. He had been aware of the soldier's continued revelling next door, the sound of carousing downstairs, the gush of the woman's urine into the chamber pot followed by her hurried laving. This brought his attention back to her, as he watched her in the corner of the room pour water from a gleaming brass pitcher into a basin. The reflection of her candle-lit image entranced him a moment, and she, sensing his observant stillness, turned and looked at him distrustfully. Without saying anything, she extinguished the candle and left the room.

He was aware of a presence in the room.

'Gerard?' he called into the dark. Soon the figure was upon him, turning Johannes around in his arms, his hands on his behind; then the boy was brought up against the man's chest, where he was held there strongly, unable to move. His panic had subsided. These hands were gentle, if determined, stroking his hair, and they went down where Johannes had been afraid to play for very long. The tickling of his behind was not unpleasant. Only the man's beery breath and moustache grated. When the man had finished, Johannes reached out, holding his waist, and put his hand into the man's breeches. It was as if it was the other Johannes, he told himself.

Then, a loud knock on the door, and the man moved, bounding across the room.

'Are you there, Gerard?' a drunken slur came from the soldier.

Gerard did not answer, but he waited, leaving only when the soldier had wandered off.

Johannes lay in the bed for some minutes, then dressed and went outside. On the landing, a sequence of eye-lines from below defined his progress along, then down to the tavern proper. The laughing and carousing seemed louder than before, as if individual words were separating themselves from different conversations to join and gather around him. He wanted to avoid all eye contact but a maid forced him to respond. Not knowing if he would see Gerard again, he ordered another drink. Only that way could he be forgotten. At this moment of despair he noticed for the first time the roundel in a window on the other side of the tavern. He stared into the dark circle until he could see one image and one image only, of the one person who might save him and yet who would surely never accept what he had experienced that night: the face of Catharina. She must never know, however mitigating his circumstances might have been.

He never saw the soldier again, and did not see Gerard for many years. The woman's face had already sunk into the depths of the night so that that persistent, yet benevolent, glass-framed image of Catharina had already replaced it in his mind. Though what would replace another, darker image, he could not say. He returned alone to the academy. The tavern was closed. He had never known the place so dark and still. Whenever he had lain in bed, it was always with a sense that life downstairs and outside was continuing, that he had not used up the full potential of the day. He was less diligent than the other pupils who by candle attempted to perfect with the mind's recollection drawings of forms witnessed earlier in the day. He did not value drawings, and so could summon up little motivation to develop any but the most rudimentary outlines, and even these lacked that necessary third dimension so close to his heart. He sensed that something must take their place; perhaps, finally, there would be no intermediary between the object captured by the eye and the paint that trapped and incorporated it.

The darkness and silence of the hallway and stairs at Van Loo's was like a rebuke. He felt shunned by the interior that he had so grudgingly come to like. He was alone, as if suspended in this dark. Thoughts, friendship, light, were withheld him now. The house's occupants were not sleeping; they were colluding in their absence from the light and from him. He would have to put everything together into the correct pattern, re-align it with purpose and infuse it with studied light. What he was now, what was in him, which had not been in him earlier that evening and since his arrival, and what was gone from him, would have to be hidden, covered, painted over, reassembled.

He passed the solitary cupid with its solitary sign. Only one lover. Only one. Illogical sparks of colour were firing off at him from the untenanted space of his room, and he felt a reverberation of form, of shifting surfaces, the percussion of form, a kind of dance, and in all this he almost grasped contentment. Yet that slipped away, out, as if the negating, avaricious night were still slowly sucking out the remains of light left over, as if such patinas of light had slept till now.

It was night and he was empty. He would force himself to forget these events, just as he would not remember the woman's face for such a long time that when it returned he would deny its appearance in this earlier life.

## Chapter three

Even on his return from Utrecht, two years after that time in Amsterdam, Johannes still felt as if a screen was separating him from knowledge, as if he were forever the onlooker, as if his hand was still visible on the curtain that heralded the scene before him. He felt as if his hand was within the frame, yet his presence did nothing to bridge foreground and background. He had come closer, certainly, but his view was still too close, still a blur. And that too, for a while, could have been said of his view of Delft as he approached it by canal for the first time in two years.

Delft, that day, was the familiar mixture of floating, tentative Dutch light and solid blocks of Italian ochre. The quayside seemed more active than ever before, and the absence of prostitutes was noticeable. The place was cleaner. Yet for Johannes there was no longer the accompanying hand of his father or his sister, though he felt confident that another would soon take its place.

Now a different memory competed with those of Amsterdam, from his time in Utrecht with Bloemaert, the counterpart of the one glimpsed at Bramer's house in Delft. He remembered the pewter-lidded pitcher, which had stood on the rug covering the table. Above the virginal hung the ebony-framed mirror, which would for him always occupy the same place. High up in the corner of the room was a biblical painting as well. Then there was the red Spanish leather chair, with a bass viol somewhere on the floor, invariably discarded. And a second figure would be present in the room, a man with whom Johannes seldom communicated. At the centre of all this was Catharina Bolnes, now recognisably a woman, though only seventeen. And her face, her face, disembodied, forever shifting over that mercury surface, a surface of desire, as if it were liquid, a wilful, unstable element opening itself to whims of observation.

And yet he had won her heart there, in Utrecht. Or had begun to win it. There was still her mother, and his own parents. His return to Delft—the actual place less real than the Delft in his mind, the city contracted and sharpened by distance and time as if seen through a convex mirror—would see the process through. Yet did he not expect too much from the middling town and from the promise of his talent?

To be sure, Amsterdam had left the young apprentice Vermeer dissatisfied. It was true that he had been able to see more examples of other paintings, especially Italian, than ever before, but he had made few friends and had never felt at home there. He was at once constricted by the canals and crowded out by the people until he felt like drawing himself in like one of the many narrow buildings standing hidden in shadow.

Utrecht had offered other possibilities. He had studied under the well-known artist, Abraham Bloemaert. It was here that Johannes spoke to Catharina Bolnes once more. Catharina, it turned out, was distantly related to Bloemaert, and was then paying a brief visit on behalf of her mother.

On that day at Bloemaert's now, indirect as his sight of her was, he was emboldened to speak. On this occasion he saw her first in the mirror as she stood at the virginal. There was no one else in the room. She carried on playing even when he entered, not looking up. He stood at the back, aware of himself reflected in the mirror. When she stopped playing, he introduced himself, and she, as modesty bade, withdrew without a word.

He was to see her only once more in Utrecht; on that occasion, some months later, he would make his proposal.

Overcome by a sudden melancholy, shortly before he was to be reunited with Digna, Reynier, and Gertruy, Johannes sought somewhere dark yet comforting. He entered Margareta Huybrechts's bookshop on the Oude Langendijck, with no particular goal in mind. The lure of books, ever since his discovery of De Vries' *Perspective* in Rietwijck's library, had remained with him, though the longing these costly, delicate volumes exercised over him was seldom satisfied.

Now, back in Delft, he felt safe. He was not likely to find the kind of books that would be useful to him in his work— Vignola's treatise: *Le Due Regole*; a De Vries, a Hendrick Hondius—and thus be tempted; the town was still provincial, it had not woken up yet to such developments. Amsterdam had been a constant torture, an enticement in this and many other respects.

It seemed Margareta was on some errand and Johannes browsed undisturbed for some time. Then he noticed how the light, coming in from the solitary yet wide high window, seemed to vibrate. Distracted, he looked round to see the source of this strange illumination, and realised a storm was threatening. When he looked back, he was startled to find Margareta standing only a few feet from him, holding a folio in her hands. She said nothing as she handed it over to him, and he took the heavy book in silence and examined it. In wine-coloured, finely-tooled leather binding, it was a 1644 translation of Cesare Ripa's *Iconologia*. Johannes had wanted this volume for some time. As his fingers revealed the series of spare woodcut engravings of allegorical figures, he was immediately immersed in another world that carried no ambiguity.

'But how?' he started to say.

Margareta took him by the arm.

'It is my present, young master Johannes.'

He looked back to the opened page that showed the two-headed *Theology* sitting on her star-encrusted globe. It was not the craft that he admired; he could not tolerate such blunt workings of line; it was, rather, the concentrated gazes of these emblematic forms.

Outside, he could finally face his parents.

*But you have achieved so little*, the familiar voice said inside him.

The storm clouds that had formed as he browsed in the shop were now one enormous cowl pulled over the town. On the Great Market Square the light was brutal, irised into an inquisitor's stark black stare. He was suddenly burdened by the thought that perhaps there would never in fact be a day when he could push the darkness back and control the light as, from the deepest part of him, he wished. And yet he must be optimistic; if he could succeed in convincing his parents about his intentions for Catharina, he knew he would succeed in life.

The deluge hit the square with the suddenness and force of a horse bolting, giving experienced marketers no time to prepare themselves. Within minutes, empty boxes, fruit, wood and canvas pieces from stalls, lottery tickets, children's toys, gentlemen's canes, and other objects were flying across the square. Johannes caught a swathe of canvas and held it tight around his head. Blown across the square like a kite, he was afraid even to cross the small distance from where he was to Mechelen. He decided to take shelter instead under the portico of the entrance to the Town Hall. Huddled there with his townsfolk, he felt strangely humble. The returning, triumphant artist! An expected fanfare! He studied them and the struggling stallholders, reluctant to leave their wares exposed, and he was reminded once more that as a painter he did not have a theme. Exteriors appealed to him less and less.

The rain stopped abruptly, the clouds scooped out of the sky by a benevolent god. Directly opposite them, it was as if the windows of the Nieuwe Kerk were on fire, a sea of screaming vermilion eyes. A few of the company crossed themselves, and Johannes looked around at them with curiosity. Yes, how will I be protected on the Day? And then this glassy sight was accompanied by an impossible, sulphurous smell. Yet it was not coming from the church. Had there been lightning? Yes, lightning had struck, he heard someone say. But then the smell was gone and forgotten as quickly as it had come, and the various members of this hastily assembled group began to disperse.

On his way towards Mechelen, Johannes continued to keep his eye on the windows of the tower, expecting a waning of the red reflection's intensity, but it seemed rather to grow stronger and defy the angled correction of his retreat. When a crack and splintering sound shot across the air, he ducked, thinking the tower had been hit. He heard a howl and a scream, then nothing, except the sound of market sellers and officials picking up the debris from the storm. Looking up, he saw the steeple whole and strong, its new sandy stone now soaking up the orange, unmediated light.

The tavern had changed, though where that change lay was hard to discern. Certainly, it lacked light and there were new paintings. He could not see his parents, yet the place was crowded with people as if unaware of the storm that had so recently raged outside.

He thought back to his father's strange, muted leavetaking in Amsterdam. Though he had corresponded with him since that time through Digna, the feeling remained that Johannes had in some way transgressed. Whether this was in some part due to Digna's poverty of expression, he did not know.

His father's feelings, already indirect in themselves, had thus, during his absence, been reported as if doubly refracted. Surely they had not forgotten his coming? And yet, if they were gone, where was this good-hearted atmosphere coming from?

Looking around the inn's clients, in one corner he noticed a man who momentarily looked his way. Unlike the gentlemen around him, he was casually dressed, his gaze both penetrating and open. His companion, more distinguished-looking, seemed anxious to hold the other's attention. The first had evidently been distracted from a very involved discussion. They could only be artists, Johannes decided.

Walking towards the bar, Johannes did not recognise the maid, nor she him. Then far away in the small back kitchen, as if the lintel and jamb of the door framed them in this position, he suddenly registered the scene. Digna, Reynier, Gertruy, her husband Anthony, Tanneken, Margareta, and De Langue sat in silence, immobile. Awaiting him. Uncertainty dissolved into celebration, letting him in, leading him back.

The silver spoon assumed a pearly sheen as it rose to meet Digna's lips, and Johannes felt an unreasonable sense of shame. His mother, whom he loved, was disappointed with him. Everyone was dressed for his homecoming, but it suited her less than the others.

'Catharina Bolnes.'

Digna was now reiterating the name, her head turning awkwardly, as if the movement were a necessary discomfort brought about by producing the word.

'She hasn't said yes,' Johannes said by way of mitigation.

'She's a Catholic.'

Reynier's fruit knife dropped to the table, as if in oblique warning, but Johannes did not feel the old physical threat. It was not so much that he had grown stronger during his absence as that Reynier had become thinner, less ruddy, as if some of his substance had seeped out like paint from one of the pig's bladder pouches used for storing colours.

'Come, woman, we have covered this ground before,' he said. 'You know what family she comes from.'

'Father, that's not why . . .' Johannes began.

'And she's older.' Digna would not relent. 'This is what comes of your schemes.' She was speaking to Reynier, but avoiding his eyes.

Though Digna had relented and entered into a project of preparing the inn for the reception of guests from a different class and faith, he could not see her for some time. However, during this period of scrubbing and cleaning and polishing the inn for the impending visit, another problem was solved; Johannes took over Gertruy's vacated room for his studio, while keeping his own bedroom as well.

The next morning, as the market sellers and soldiers from the town militia helped clear up after the storm, he and Reynier set about acquiring new materials, including an easel, some strainers, a stone slab for grinding colours, and blinds. On these trips they would occasionally glimpse Catharina, but Reynier would say nothing. Sometimes Johannes would attempt to move their search towards the Catholic district, his stratagem barely disguised, as if to acknowledge that the otherwise identical façades of their buildings were now ready to reveal the true nature of their inhabitants' faith and way of life, like earlier tracings pushing themselves to the upper surface of a canvas.

A few days later, on a similar excursion with Reynier, Johannes again saw the two men he had noticed in the inn on the day of his return to Delft. He was reminded, in their curious pairing, of his Amsterdam tutor Van Loo and Gerard Terborch. Reynier's enthusiasm was palpable.

'Now, Johannes, we have a great opportunity here.'

The two artists veered towards them just as Johannes was beginning to fear they might try to avoid the innkeeper.

'Dear Reynier,' said the well-dressed one, taking his hand without hesitation. Johannes noticed the man's long, spidery eyelashes, which seemed to exist to draw in light and a wider view. 'I take it this is the talented son you have spoken of so much?'

Reynier nodded, making no attempt to mask his pride.

'Johannes, you have the honour of meeting Samuel van Hoogstraten and Carel . . .' he hesitated, shifting his diminished weight impatiently, 'Fabritius,' the other man said.

'Yes, I'm sorry. Masters Hoogstraten and Fabritius have both been pupils of Rembrandt van Rijn. There is much that you could learn from them.'

This comment seemed to open up a seam from which Hoogstraten's enthusiasm suddenly poured. 'I have just been looking at our dear friend Carel's box. Quite a wonder.'

'Box?' Johannes queried. Reynier appeared slightly nervous at his son's intervention.

'I will tell you later,' Reynier said.

'No, no, dear Reynier. I can explain.' He looked directly at Johannes. 'A perspective box is a rectangular or triangular box that allows you to look into a scene as if you are in the very space yourself. Carel has been showing me his experiment with a triangular box, an interior.'

Johannes' interest was hard to disguise, and Hoogstraten appeared to want to ease an introduction between him and Fabritius.

'I would show you my own box, but I don't have an example of my work in Holland, and, besides, I am leaving Delft in a few days. But,' he continued to Carel, 'what if young Master Vermeer paid you a visit, Carel?'

Carel appeared to suppress a certain reluctance. Johannes understood. He must be wondering what he would gain from contact with the apprenticed son of an innkeeper, who by all accounts was only just managing to keep his business together.

'You are welcome,' he finally said to Johannes. 'I live near the gunpowder magazine. You know it?'

Johannes nodded. He had been in the unsavoury district, where he had seen drunken fights and paupers pressganged into voyages from Delfshaven.

'That is settled, then,' concluded Hoogstraten almost as if a contract had been signed. 'When I return, dear Reynier, I look forward to enjoying your hospitality.'

On their return to the house, a workman was outside white-varnishing the wood of the window frames. Inside, this spurt of activity continued as Tanneken and the new maid set about cleaning the tavern, urging their diligence into gaps and onto surfaces that Johannes hardly recalled noticing before. A kitchen boy had even been brought off the streets to help while the double task of cleaning the tavern and preparing the food for Catharina and her mother, Maria Thins, got under way.

Later that day, as he walked aimlessly about the house, Johannes saw beyond the door to the rear cooking kitchen where broad-hipped Tanneken was lifting the great earthenware milk jug so lightly, almost as if it were a baby. His reverie was disturbed by the kitchen boy, who appeared from another room to snatch up a cumin-encrusted roll, which he broke open roughly in his hands and layered thickly with butter. The sudden release of that fresh, seedy-doughy smell wafted over to Johannes, not only disturbing the beauty of this scene, but also making him hungry at the same time.

That night he dreamt of a house foreign to him in its furnishings but familiar in all the sensations it evoked. It was a house of a higher order. Its rooms were nested within one another at night, only to be drawn out again during the day. It was a house where many paintings seemed to take him on a journey through his life; where certain objects, while not in the ostentatious abundance of a wealthy burgher, were nevertheless each placed to display an aspect of one of his desires. There was the marble of tiles, the pewter of a jug, the lead mullion of a window, or the blue of a chair's upholstery. He was taking an inventory of this house, whose hall, whose many kitchens, whose bedrooms were leading him to one undeniable goal. In a room he saw her, older, fuller, forcing a new life inside her to the very extremes of her light, turquoise-veined skin. In his parents' canopy bed she was bearing his child, and she was looking at him.

Carel's studio was dirty, disordered, and cold. He offered Johannes a glass of wine and stared into the younger artist's eyes as if he had just noticed an interesting fleck of something there. He seemed to be looking at Johannes from the end of a long tunnel, but without the intervening loss of scale.

Despite the general shabbiness, the studio was light, giving, on one side, onto a yard paved with flagstones. They might have been in uninhabited countryside, except for the closeness of the canal on which the main studio window looked. Carel talked of Amsterdam, of Rembrandt, above all, of darkness.

'Too dark, much too dark,' he repeated.

'Is that why you came here?'

'What?' Carel said, put off track.

'For the light. The light here is special, don't you think?'

Carel looked at him enigmatically, twirling the end of one of his long locks, as if he were considering the charms of a young woman.

'Ah, yes, the light,' he replied, then remained silent.

Lost for words, Johannes looked around the studio. On a workbench he noticed what seemed to be some kind of paper model, and next to these some panels.

'What is that?' he asked, drawing closer.

Carel's distracted air was suddenly gone. 'Why, this is my box!' he exclaimed.

The model was made up of two square pieces of paper placed so as to make a V, an open triangle. On these pieces Johannes saw a lightly-pencilled perspective drawing that showed the interior of a house, with a view through a hallway into various rooms, including a kitchen, a bedroom, and a garden. There were paintings on either wall of the hallway, the lightly-drawn figure of a maid, and the shadow of a gentleman in the bedroom. Johannes had seen many such pretty interior scenes, but this one held his attention for another reason; it did not make complete sense. The floor tiles at one point proceeded impossibly upwards, and one painting was hanging on two adjoining walls at the same time.

'The scene in itself is of no importance,' Carel said, and Johannes felt a curious sense of relief. 'But, if we look here,' he continued, drawing Johannes' attention to two walnut panels, which Johannes saw were on a temporary hinge, 'you can find an idea of what it might offer.'

Now Carel took up the panels, lightly stuck the paper squares to each panel, then covered the front view, along with the roof of the box, with a sheet of translucent paper so that the entire model formed a triangular box. The view in, however, was not completely blocked. Halfway up the front panel there was a small hole. The older artist invited the younger to look through. Immediately, Johannes saw the purpose of the experiment, and released an involuntary gasp of wonder. He was standing in the room and looking in from outside at the same time! The skewed perspective and the distortions were almost gone: the floor no longer inclined upwards, and the painting was hanging normally, from only one wall.

'How did you do it?'

Saying nothing, Carel began to disassemble the box, taking off the top and front covers. With his finger he pointed to the lines that, looked at from above, without the discipline of the peephole, refused to create a logical image.

'The rule is simple. If two lines meet at an angle, they will not appear to be continuous. But if they are viewed along the plane that contains them both, they will *appear* to be straight and continuous. The same is true for lines above and below the horizon. Now—' Carel broke off for effect, enjoying Johannes' wide-eyed look of scarcely-suppressed admiration.

'Now, in theory the viewing position could be anywhere along this line containing the peephole, but in practice it works best only from a certain position. And it's a difficult business to find that point. I have not quite succeeded yet.' He smiled at Johannes.

'So how do you construct it? What is the procedure?'

Carel bridled. 'What, you expect me to tell you all my secrets?'

Johannes was taken aback. He had gone too far.

Carel's smile returned.

'It was a jest. Now, imagine we have yet to determine the ideal position of the hole.'

Carel took some translucent paper and placed this over the two side panel drawings on the inside of the box in such a way that blurred images came into view. He brought over some pieces of string, which he attached to points on either panel. Asking Johannes to hold the strands steady, Carel looked along the lines of sight that the strings created and adjusted the imaginary viewing point until he was satisfied, fixing it on the temporary front panel, which he now stuck back on. With the two ends of string joined at this temporary eye-point, he moved the ends of the strings to different locations, forming different lines and pyramids of sight.

It seemed that Carel was showing him how the ends of the further points of this triangle corresponded to a number of stages on the perspective drawing, often those that depicted tiles, where lines on either panel met at the join at the back of the box. During this second operation Carel showed slight annoyance as he altered one point along a line by piercing the translucent paper with a pen so that it left a mark on the perspective drawing underneath.

'That line will have to be changed again. And so it goes on.'

Johannes felt a tremor go through him. Was he sure that he had understood? He thought of De Vries' multiplying views, and a tingle ran along the veins of his hands. And the light, the light!

Carel noticed the young man's sudden restlessness.

'Come, let us sit by the water.'

Carel brought with him some red-rind cheese and a knife whose wandering reflection about the yard Johannes absently followed. 'Did you learn about the box from Rembrandt?'

Carel let out an exaggerated laugh, almost choking on the cheese, which he had to spit out. It landed on Johannes' leg.

'Rembrandt was not interested in perspective. That comes from Hoogstraten.'

'Rembrandt will teach you paint, paint, paint. Paint from the mind,' Carel continued. 'But it was all too dark.'

This talk of the Amsterdam master seemed to return Carel to his earlier state of melancholy brooding.

They spent some minutes gazing into the canal. Then Carel jumped up.

'Wait. I have something to show you.'

Carel went into his studio and came back out again with a wooden box.

'Do you know what this is?' he asked Johannes.

Johannes had not seen such a thing before. From one end of the box emerged a small cylinder surmounted by a lens. At the other end, on the upper side, there was a misted glass plate. At first he could not see anything in the glass until Carel turned it away from himself and directed it across the canal to the building opposite. Johannes saw how the image of the house seemed to present itself to him more insistently than it would have done on the brightest day of summer without such an intermediary.

Johannes marvelled once more at the device, and asked, 'What do you use it for?'

Upon this, Carel put the box under his arm and beckoned him to go outside with him. 'Come, you'll see.'

He followed Carel for some time till they reached the corner of the Vrouwenrecht and Oude Langendijck. Across the canal stood the Nieuwe Kerk. To the right of the church there was a cluster of houses; to the left, he became slowly aware, the seated figure of an instrument maker. Whether he was selling his wares or resting, Johannes could not have said, but he seemed involved in contemplation so serene that nothing disturbed him, least of all the sight of these two artists standing over their strange box.

'See,' said Carel as he guided Johannes to look at the image in the glass, 'see how the lens enables you to encompass everything in view, right up to the thoughtful gentleman outside our range of vision.'

Upon these words Carel whisked away the box as if to make more dramatic the gulf between what Johannes' naked eye would have put within the frame of a painting and what this device would allow him to. The church, which the box had made beautifully, intriguingly distant, was now back, dominating their natural view.

'Yes, I see.'

'That is why,' Carel continued, 'my next painting will be called "View *in* Delft" and not "View *of* Delft".'

Johannes hummed his admiration with a line of words that, though they trailed out in logical connection, and Carel nodded in agreement, had at this moment in fact no connection with the workings of his mind.

On his way back, as he skirted the Nieuwe Kerk, Johannes pondered what it was he had not felt able to express. It was not the distortions of perspective or the encompassing point of view that truly interested him. It was, rather, the possibilities that such a device might have. Did this device indeed not have the potential to highlight areas of almost otherworldly shade of which the naked eye was usually unconscious, and allow a draughtsman to reassemble these passages to his liking? And yet, at the same time, he felt there was a mathematical precision at work here, a tangible accuracy that would be borne out even by the work of the Italians. If only, he felt, his ability in the field of mathematics and geometry were better, he could have proved that the one system complemented and proved the other.

Nothing was said of the absence of Catharina's father. Maria made it known that Willem Bolnes did not object to the prospective marriage, yet only on this day did Johannes realise the strength of the obstacle he faced in Catharina's mother.

It was his first real opportunity to study her. Unlike the rounded comfort of his own mother's features, Maria Thins' were sharp, as if an invisible net were drawn over them, fixed tight at the back by an inner determination. It was fortunate that her almost rodent-like face had hardly any echo in Catharina's, except perhaps in the serious set of her eyes and mouth.

With the exception of these guests-of-honour, Maria and Catharina, it was the same company as it had been on the day of Johannes' arrival. But there were additions, additions that fascinated and disturbed Johannes at the same time. The fluted wine glasses, which were difficult to drink from, and which he was afraid he might break, so delicate and thin were they; a new faïence set with a tulip flower motif; a sugar bowl of Chinese design that did not belong in any way with these other objects; and perhaps the most startling of all, the damask tablecloth, which previously he had seen only as his father's material or in Bramer's and Bloemaert's houses. Only the silver was familiar, but it was so well polished that he could see his, and Catharina's, reflection in it.

Maria Thins surprised everyone with her first words.

'I know from our dear friend Abraham Bloemaert that your son shows great promise,' she said, directing her tensed profile at Digna, whose sigh was, for Johannes, humiliatingly audible. Yet this did not perplex him as much as the observation that Maria Thins was not taking any notice of Reynier.

'Master Bloemaert has said as much,' Digna answered, then seemed self-conscious, as if this comment were showing a failure to acknowledge Juffrouw Thins' compliment.

Everyone seemed to hang on Maria's response.

'Then it will not be long before he enters the Guild?'

Johannes looked hopefully at his parents. Reynier startled Maria, firstly by clearing his throat, then with his next words, 'We have what is necessary, Juffrouw Thins.'

'I am glad to hear it.' She took up her spoon, seemingly satisfied, then added, 'I simply will *not* countenance a miserable future for Catharina. You have probably heard about Bolnes and that wastrel son of mine?'

There was an appreciative but respectful rumble of acknowledgement around the table, along with a mischievous smile from Tanneken.

'You know that Bolnes beat me when I was pregnant with Catharina? And that he beat the poor child herself?'

Involuntarily, Johannes let drop his spoon, which clanged like a gong as if to usher in the next course.

'I won't rest easy until he is placed in a house of correction,' Maria added. And at this, for the first time in Johannes' time at Mechelen, lobster was served.

The illness came suddenly, cutting Reynier down as if he had been clubbed from behind in a bad-tempered game of kolf on the ice. Digna took on the burden of the extra work without complaint, and when he was confined to bed, soiling the sheets and helpless, she took them and cleaned them herself.

Johannes was allowed only the briefest instance of clarity from his father during this time. Without his father declaring it, he knew that Reynier was ready to die, that this humiliation was enough; he knew, too, that his father now considered his son well able to make his way in the world.

On that last occasion when they spoke, with that innocent raucousness coming from downstairs in the inn, and the end-of-afternoon light retreating from the room, Reynier took Johannes' hand.

'There'll be some debts, Johannes. But small. Forgive me.'

'No matter,' Johannes replied.

'The paintings are yours to do with as you please. Don't ... don't look down on my efforts.'

'No, I have nothing but respect for you, father.'

Then Reynier began to mutter words that Johannes could not understand. Johannes looked to the door, reluctant to leave him on his own. What would he do were his father to die now, while they were alone?

'Mother!' he shouted. 'Mother!'

They would never hear it amongst all that noise. He let his father's hand slip away from his, and rushed downstairs.

He arrived back with Gertruy a few minutes later. He knew it would be too late, and he could not bear to hear them wail. It would be the first death in their neat, tight family. But Digna, when she came, sat down calmly on Reynier's right, Gertruy to his left, and asked him to call the predikant.

Part two:
*The Shifting Surface of Desire*

'It is not possible to describe for you the beauty of it in words: all painting is dead in comparison; for here is life itself, or something more noble, if only it did not lack words.'

> *Constantijn Huygens, speaking of the camera obscura, in* De briefwisseling *("Correspondence") from Svetlana Alpers'* The Art of Describing: Dutch Art in the Seventeenth Century *(1983)*

*The Secret Journal of Balthasar de Monconys, pertaining to the extraordinary events surrounding some days in the life of the painter, Johannes Vermeer of Delft, as read by his son on the author's death.*

Lyons, April 1665

My Dear Ferdinand,

    I hope I have your trust in putting these speculative thoughts to the page, for any disclosure of the contents of this document will surely lead to our name being sullied forever, if not to your own life being subject to extreme danger. I beseech you upon my imminent death to destroy what you hold in your hands; yet I feel that I cannot go to our dear Lord without communicating to you the secret knowledge, which I have been forbidden to publish, and which calls into question all that I hold true. Yet the subject of my discourse here is, I am convinced, a person so singular and benign in his aims and mission that I do not believe my rôle in this matter will serve any cause but that of the greater good. So, without further peroration, I, Balthasar de Monconys, shall begin, in the form of this testament, the alternative journal of my travels in that strange enigma that is the prospering Holland of today.

    It pains me to start from a position of retrospection,

as I should like to talk of the glorious future of a great talent. But I do not know how long he will live, how much he will achieve. So I must start with my first visits, which are the reported, official visits, after that quickly to progress to those others which I have till now forborne to disclose.

I first entered Delft on the 3rd day of August, 1663, unaccompanied, and slightly preoccupied with other matters. My dear friend and fellow enthusiast of the human sciences Monsieur Huygens having been indisposed to receive me as arranged, I decided to include the small and wealthy town of Delft in my itinerary. I had travelled there by barge, for once oblivious to worries of a religious or artistic nature. I had in mind nothing more taxing than a brief perusal of De Keyser's Town Hall and the Nieuwe Kerk.

However, I was delighted to discover a clean and beautifully proportioned town, where, above all, light and the disposition of the streets and buildings was so rarely combined as to produce a harmony such as I had not in all my travels yet seen. It seemed remarkable to me too that, in a town where the military aspect was so present, peace nevertheless had a firm footing; the vagaries of the sea seemed the only dangers. I departed from the town feeling that I was leaving behind a quietly dozing spaniel. It was with consternation, then, that I learned from Monsieur Huygens only after my return to The Hague of a celebrated painter, known as Johannes Vermeer, who resides in Delft. I was, of course, welcomed by Monsieur Huygens, and given ample opportunity to see his incomparable collection of pictures. Then a fortuitous occurrence came about. After attending a sermon by a fellow countryman of mine, a certain Père Léon, I was invited to dine with him. During our conversation I learned that he intended travelling to

Delft along with a Lieutenant-Colonel Gentillo, a member of our faith. Their aim was to visit one of the 'hidden churches' of which I had heard so much and an example of which I had seen in Rotterdam. One week later, therefore, I was happy to join my brethren on their journey.

The weather on that second visit was not so accommodating; the air was humid, and the clouds seemed to hang over the town in sullen resentment of our intrusion. To add to this inauspicious beginning, I must confess that Père Léon and I had exchanged a slight difference of opinion over where we should visit first. He was naturally for the church, but as we had planned only on staying the afternoon and I had accepted to dine with them on our return to The Hague, this would have left even less time for our calling on Monsieur Vermeer should he be engaged in some work and ask us to come back later.

The church was no more than a back room in a house with a table covered with a rug and a representation of the Last Judgement behind it, the whole serving as an altar. Yet it was fascinating in its modesty; in the time we were there, there was a steady stream of worshippers, who unfortunately had to be turned away due to our presence as they wished to give us a privileged tour. Meanwhile, I confess, the excitement of the idea of viewing Monsieur Vermeer's work was all the while growing ever greater in me. It was only after some extended conversation with the newly instituted Van Beke that Père Léon reluctantly agreed to make our presence known to the neighbouring master.

Our first attempt was to no purpose. Upon knocking on his door, we were met by a sturdy-looking maid whose attention was continually divided between us and some task or other, which necessitated her constantly looking back down the marble-tiled hall. Then, through her skirts and apron, there emerged a young girl, curly-locked and shy, who held onto the maid's strong thigh as if she might fall away at any moment. The maid and girl were soon joined by a pale-complexioned woman of thirty years or thereabouts, who was possessed of a full face and figure. She smiled as if she had foreknowledge of our diverse reasons for being there, but in doing this she revealed a curiosity which surprised us in a housewife.

'Do we have the pleasure of calling on Juffrouw Vermeer?' Père Léon began.

'You do. If it is my husband you seek, he is in his painting room.'

Père Léon looked around curiously, first at Gentillo and then at myself, as if we might provide an answer.

'Would it be possible to see your husband? We have come from . . .'

'Certainly. But his room is across the Great Market in the Mechelen Inn.'

We thanked her and left for the inn. I was a little taken aback by her manner, a little confused that the mere wife of a painter could in fact appear completely at her ease with someone of Père Léon's standing, but I was nevertheless full of anticipation.

The inn was quieter than I had expected. I could not but notice immediately the class of clients, evidently painters of some standing and military officers of rank, judging from their bright sashes and well-tailored jackets. We were greeted warmly by an old woman who, from time to time, looked down at her apron as if to check its state of cleanliness.

'Good day, sirs.'

'Good day,' Père Léon replied. 'We are looking for a Monsieur Vermeer.'

'My son? He's working. I'm sure he'll be honoured, but I shouldn't like to disturb him. Of late there have been so many interruptions . . .'

These last words she said with the manner of someone attempting to extract herself from the orbit of a bothersome insect.

'May we then take on that burden?' I offered, anxious to ease the situation.

'I'm afraid he's very particular about such things.'

She paused a while, then said, as if our status had no bearing on the matter, 'I suppose I shall have to ask the maid.'

She made a gesture to a serving girl, who went to the back of the inn and disappeared from view.

We stood there a little awkwardly perhaps, but my curiosity was captured as my eyes, which had been following the maid, were stopped by the sight of a small scene at the back of the inn, of people passing beyond the canal, of a small lime tree, and the sight of a young child playing there by the water's edge. There was nothing so remarkable in this scene except that I thought for that brief moment I was gazing at a beautiful piece of art. It occurred to me that for all the city's prettiness till now on display to my eyes, I had not had such thoughts before.

I was brought out of this reverie by the reappearance of the maid, who, whilst displaying the most affable deference to Père Léon and myself, was evidently in no hurry to convey her message.

To the painter's mother and us at the same time, she said simply, 'Master Vermeer is pleased to see the gentlemen.'

As we followed the maid, I was most engaged by the distribution of the rooms, which led almost imperceptibly into others and particularly struck by the darkness of the corridors, which barely afforded enough light by which to see the many pictures about the house. I am afraid that I dallied somewhat over a few, to Père Léon's and Gentillo's impatience.

There was, however, to be a further prologue to our introduction to this master. As we approached his room, a young lady, dressed most finely in a bodice of lemon yellow silk with black velvet borders, a black skirt of the same material, and beneath this, another skirt of crimson cloth, passed by us. She had, for all the world, the outward show of a woman of standing, yet she failed to greet us in a commensurate manner, preferring instead to sink her gaze to the floor. Père Léon turned to me, baffled, whilst Gentillo gazed wistfully after her.

The young woman had left the door open so that we could already see, as if it were illicitly, into part of the room. Within this rectangular view, on the wall, was a rather old-fashioned *Roman Charity*, in which Pero suckled her manacled father Cimon.

I was aware of a fusty smell and, mixed in with it, a slightly sulphurous taint. Monsieur Vermeer himself was seated on a painter's stool, working on the canvas before him. He turned an interested welcome to us, though he was in no way overawed, as I had feared he might be by someone such as myself accompanied by a Catholic priest and an officer. I should say, from his moonish complexion, he was in his early thirties, although in this extremely open, innocent face there was nevertheless discernible a surface of worldliness.

'Mijn Heer Vermeer, we are honoured to have this opportunity to visit you,' I started. Père Léon translated.

But in the kindest way, Monsieur Vermeer waved a hand and replied in simple French, which surprised us all, that translation would not be necessary.

'I pray, Mijn Heer Vermeer, that this visit does not inconvenience you,' I continued. 'You see, I come to your renowned town of Delft for the second time this week, and, well, on that first occasion I neglected . . . In short, please accept my apologies. I had a busy itinerary. However, on my return, I was recommended by Mijn Heer Huygens,' (here Monsieur Vermeer raised an eyebrow in acknowledgement), 'to pay you this visit.'

Before I could continue, Père Léon added what I, in my impatience, had neglected to mention:

'We are indeed grateful to you, sir, but I am certain it will not surprise you to know that I felt it my duty to welcome Father van Beke and to see your marvellous, hidden church.'

Père Léon's words were followed by an uncharacteristic chortle of excitement, which amused us all and helped a great deal to break down the formality of this meeting.

'And most welcomed we were by your neighbours in that place,' I added.

'*I* am most honoured also,' Monsieur Vermeer returned, 'that you have made such a journey on my behalf. But I think I must disappoint you. I have no pictures of my own here to show you.'

I do not think I was able to smother my sigh of frustration and hoped that I had not offended him. For their part, Père Léon and the Lieutenant turned towards one another in some embarrassment, and we looked about the studio a little, as if searching for the remains of evidence hastily removed. Might we yet be able to rescue something from our trip? I could not help but make a note in my mind of the simplicity and sparseness of the disposition of the room, its three bays of windows, a Spanish leather chair with its pattern of yellow and blue lozenges, and a simple mirror. Then there was another pattern, without which no Dutch home would be a home, it seemed to me—the tiles, which were small and alternated from reddish-pink to greenish-blue in colour.

I naturally sought the painted counterparts of these elements in what I took to be the master's underdrawing, executed in umber on a grey ground, yet I was intrigued as I searched in vain for an exact replication of the reality before me. In the place of small tiles, I saw much larger black crosses centred by white squares decorated with dark tentacular veins. The chair was in fact upholstered in light-blue velvet. The *Roman Charity* was in Monsieur Vermeer's picture merely indicated as a thin strip, in the top right-hand corner. Most noticeable of all, moreover, was the presence on the canvas of a virginal, of which no actual example existed in the room.

I sensed Monsieur Vermeer's eyes on me, but I did not feel in a position to question him. He must have been aware of my excitement.

'If, gentlemen, you are so taken, I could suggest two possibilities. At the home of the baker Hendrick van Buyten you will find a picture of mine. Then there is a Mijn Heer van Ruijven. He has some more of my efforts, though I do not know if he is in Delft today.'

'Well, sir, we are most grateful to you. I hope that we shall have the pleasure of meeting in the future.'

To my chagrin, Père Léon and Gentillo had no interest in searching out the baker and Monsieur Vermeer's friend, so we agreed to meet outside the Town Hall at 6 a Clock in the Evening.

I did not have to look far to find the baker's shop, which had before it a short queue of women and a group of scrabbling, indigent-looking children that a young maid was attempting to chase away. As I approached, they stopped their game, looked at me warily, and ran off. The maid gestured to me thankfully, but showed surprise that I intended to enter.

To my inquiry about Monsieur van Buyten, she nodded and led me respectfully into the shop. I was startled to hear such a harsh issue of sounds from this unexpectedly fine-boned creature as she called out for the owner.

The man who emerged was ruddy-faced, thickset and most welcoming. The little Dutch I knew served me well enough to establish the reason for my visit.

Upon my pronouncing Monsieur Vermeer's name, the baker's face lit up suddenly, though his smiling expression was almost immediately interrupted by an undetectable thought. He waved a hand upwards to the wall above an open hearth where I saw a small canvas in a golden frame showing a single figure, a woman with a lute. It was very dark, too dark for close inspection, yet the yellow jacket with its fur trim still glowed; it reminded me of my first encounter with Monsieur Vermeer's wife. I remained before the picture for some time, aware of the baker's weight through the wooden floor and the plaintive sounds of cattle from the market. Suddenly, the pealing of the bells of the Nieuwe Kerk and the carriage wheels passing over the cobbled streets seemed an invasion. I must have sunk into a very noticeable absence of mind, since the baker and the maid left me standing there as they went about closing their shop.

I only became aware that those outside sounds had almost completely disappeared when Monsieur van Buyten himself closed the entrance door and looked at me expectantly.

'For such a piece, how much would you demand?' I asked.

'Six hundred guilders,' he said with absolutely no hesitation.

I could not but express my exasperation.

'Sixty guilders would be too much,' I replied, though I regretted such an incautious statement as soon as I had uttered it. However, Monsieur van Buyten seemed in no way offended.

'It is indeed a beautiful piece of art,' I said finally, in a conciliatory tone. 'But it is merely one figure, and so small.'

The baker raised his eyebrows a little, but he continued to stand there proudly as he was joined by his wife, then by the maid, who I now saw to be his daughter. I felt a sense of calm and stillness looking at them there, framed as they were in the window of their simple, clean shop. And I, too, felt a certain hopeless defeat that, with all the means at my disposal, I could no more buy such simple contentedness than I could convince myself to pay such a sum.

I returned to The Hague tired and in a sombre mood. I attempted to put disappointment from my mind, as you, my dear son, may remember. For no reason that I could understand, I suddenly found that the prettiness of this country suddenly became meaningless, and I was inclined to the English view on the art of this perplexing nation, that it in fact showed little art, since it demonstrated everyday life exactly as it took place, with no intermediary that could raise it to a higher level. It was, as I have mentioned, an art overvalued by its citizens, as if they had an insight into a favourable reception that it might in future years receive.

Yet something nevertheless intervened to hold my interest and return me by a circuitous route to what was all the time in front of my eyes. The agent of this was an acquaintance of mine, a fellow countryman, a certain

Monsieur Borry, who never tired of showing me his scientific discoveries.

Still restless after dining with Père Léon and Lieutenant-Colonel Gentillo the previous evening on our return to The Hague (I had extracted myself from their company rather early on, my enthusiasm for being with them having dissipated), I paid a visit the next evening to Monsieur Borry. When I arrived, he was even more excited than usual. His optimistic disposition, however, only served to deepen the subdued frame of mind occasioned in me by my visit to Delft.

We dined with a view out of a window onto a formal garden. I spoke of my visit to the home of Monsieur Vermeer, to whose talents Monsieur Borry seemed indifferent.

"I have heard that Constantijn Huygens values him highly,' he conceded.

'That is true. He recommended that I see him.'

'Yet you were disappointed?'

'Yes, I could only see one picture, and that not in the best circumstances.'

Despite my words, I knew as I spoke that a certain fascination had taken hold of me. 'I would like to see more, nevertheless,' I continued. 'He is presently engaged on a larger piece.'

I think I observed in my host a degree of impatience, a distraction evidenced by the constant mobility of his eyes, as if he were shifting in his seat to prevent unwanted questions. I could not help but notice him search out something beyond me in the silence and stillness of the room, from which eventually appeared his servant to fill my glass, while Monsieur Borry's own shook subtly in his hand.

He waved the servant away.

'I have information to convey to you which might explain Monsieur Vermeer's reticence.'

'Yes?'

'Monsieur Huygens could perhaps tell you more. However, it concerns something of my own work.'

At this, Monsieur Borry stood up and led me to a wall lined in gilt red leather. At first I had thought he intended to show me some craftsman's detail, until I noticed from a height of about five feet a line running vertically down the wall. He bent down a little as if to point at one of the golden arabesques there, but this was revealed to be the brass handle of a hidden door. I followed him into a small workshop. There were no windows, only a narrow chimney-like flue.

I recognised immediately the smell of carbonised substances, sulphur, and various oxides. Most outstanding was a distillation apparatus of a kind I had seen in so many similar amateur apothecaries' workshops, though this example was remarkable in the complexity of its glass structures, which themselves possessed a certain element of beauty.

A look of pride passed over Monsieur Borry's face as we surveyed the place. My eyes fell on a white powder lying in a small mound on the workbench. I could not guess at its name or provenance.

Monsieur Borry fingered the flour-like substance.

'This is my invention,' he claimed, 'a distillation of ingredients. Do not press me to disclose them to you for the present time.'

'But the practical purpose? May I enquire of that?'

'It is a result of my contact with many unknowing masters. I am still uncertain as to its efficacy. And,' he continued as he turned repeatedly in his hand a glass spatula, 'certain people already know of my secret. They come constantly, wanting the formula. But they shan't have it.'

I was sensitive to the seriousness of the matter, and I did not know Monsieur Borry for one who exaggerated. But I was becoming impatient.

'May I ask what it is for?'

'It is a chemical, a very special chemical that has the ability to trap light in the most wondrous way, giving again on paper an image that will aid the most mediocre talent. Aid, I say, not make a genius.'

Monsieur Borry took a breath, then continued, his voice rising and falling in the most unpredictable manner.

'I am not happy with the final images yet, but I am certain I can improve them.'

'This sounds a most wondrous invention,' I said with genuine enthusiasm. 'Has it been used by any master?'

Monsieur Borry gave out an amused, almost contemptuous laugh, but I thought he remained a little guarded in his response.

'No, only by myself.'

'I would love nevertheless to see an example.'

Monsieur Borry considered for a great while, but I could see that the temptation and excitement were too great for him. He went over to a cupboard in a corner of the room and drew out a small sheet of paper.

On the paper was a scene now very familiar to me, a view down the front hall, the *voorhuis*, of a wealthy Dutch house, with further views into other rooms. The hallway itself was tiled and hung with a number of pictures and a map. Light and shadow were sharply re-presented to the eye, which in turn was led to a proudly posed figure at the end of the hall. Despite this person's distance from the foreground, I easily recognised him to be Monsieur Huygens. The composition and content of this view were typical, to be sure, but its method eluded me. This small image was not on the paper but *in* the very substance of it. I can only liken the effect of it to that wondrous device, the camera obscura.

'Oh, my dear Borry, what is it here?'

'Monsieur de Monconys, it is what you see. No magic.'

I was relieved that he had used the word before me, but I could not hold back my anxiety. 'I do not doubt it, but people should see this, and when they do, they will surely ask questions.'

'It may be so, yet there is a greater matter at hand.'

'What could that be?' I asked.

'There are already people who would delight to have my formula. But not to use it.'

'Then to what purpose?'

'To destroy it.'

'But what people?'

'The guilds, or sections of them, have strange rituals, such as we do not see in France, our own beloved country. I hardly dare speak of them. I have made enemies here.'

'But please explain.'

'My dear Monconys, I can only say that they exist within the guilds. There are other names for such societies, but I decline to name them. Suffice it to say that they are like a club for erudite men of letters and science, benevolent in intention, yet with a certain power to decide on unusual matters.'

'Surely, my dear Borry, these . . . organisations that you speak of would only benefit from such a development as this?'

'Do you truly think so?'

'I see no reason to think otherwise,' I asserted.

Monsieur Borry drew in his breath.

'But think, Monsieur de Monconys, what this could mean to the masters who have studied so long to wring such effects from paint, who have learned the laborious skill needed, inherited over the centuries. And very soon it could be made naught by something requiring no skill greater than a common apothecary's. Is it not a grave matter for such people?'

'I understand,' I persisted. 'Yet the skill will nevertheless be necessary to add colour. It is surely no more than an aid. Is that not so?'

'And so may it be,' he conceded, 'but I am concerned and ill at ease. They have called on me frequently. They will not leave me alone.'

'Who are these people?'

As Monsieur Borry stared past me, I noted silently that he seemed distraught.

'I cannot tell you. You and I would most certainly face annihilation.'

I began to sense that these threatening people might perhaps be none other than the benign, patrician dignitaries of the guilds.

'How can I help you, then?' I said, a slight note of irritation entering my voice.

'I shall give you the formula and the instructions. No one will know. If pressed, I shall say I have no record of it, because that will be the truth. The decision to reveal it or not will be your own.'

'I thank you for placing such trust in me. If it is the only way that I can help you, let it be so, however much it might, I feel, be accompanied by some personal jeopardy to myself,' I said.

At this stage, dear Ferdinand, allow me to digress and to remind you of my leanings towards those discoveries and small parcels of new knowledge, which are to me as truffles to a swine. If you remember, for instance, my correspondence with a certain gentleman in England, a Mr Digby and his chemicals, in fact my curiosity about every kind of liquid or elixir, how I cannot resist my urge to investigate every microscope, thermometer or glass vessel upon which I chance, then you can understand how strong was the attraction to have in my hands this formula of which Borry spoke.

At this, Monsieur Borry went back to the cupboard, from which he took various sheets of cream-vellum paper. He drew out two pages, folded, sealed and handed them to me.

'I would add, my dear Monsieur de Monconys, I could not have expected such events to come about here in Holland, yet to have met a person of such standing, trustworthiness, and evident curiosity in natural science, and a Frenchman as well, well . . . this knowledge comforts me, as much as I am loath to let my work go . . . ah! But I must. Here!'

As he thrust them towards me, the moment the papers left his possession, I saw his features relax into an expression not so dissimilar to that serene look of relief captured by a death mask, a look accentuated by the momentary closing of his eyes. I was moved to recognise in such a good person the humbleness brought about by what I could only surmise the result of some terrible politicking.

Motioning his servant away, Monsieur Borry accompanied me to the hallway, where we stood a moment, like chess pieces separated by arbitrary spaces, shaking hands on the black-and-white marbled tiles.

Only after I had left Monsieur Borry's residence that evening did I give thought to the rôle of Constantijn

Huygens in inspiring my interest in Monsieur Vermeer. I had been distracted by Monsieur Borry, and I now considered the conjunction of my unfortunate friend's worries with that interest an undesirable and unproductive avenue to pursue. Monsieur Borry knew Huygens and Monsieur Vermeer, to be sure, yet he was nervous. Surely Monsieur Huygens' interest could not but be beneficial to Borry's cause? And if not, he in any case would seek to help and protect Monsieur Vermeer. But, these ... dealings ... whatever they may be, are not for me. I only aspire to reach the essence of the matter, which is Monsieur Vermeer's talent. I shall take care of this invention as best I can to help a fellow countryman and enthusiast of the sciences, and out of a natural, perhaps selfish curiosity, though I fear I might be diverted too long from my gentle investigation of this painter.

My uncertainty might perhaps then only be assuaged by another audience with Monsieur Huygens. Yet I could not assume that I would be granted one as a matter of course. However, I had Monseigneur le Duc de Chèvreuse, whose companion I was during this time, you may remember, and I prevailed on him to bring Monsieur Huygens' attention around to me once more. The evening that I was called to Monsieur Huygens' house I found the place empty save for one servant and, from the upper floor, the refreshing chords of a virginal played dexterously and without ostentation.

As I followed the servant to the room from which the music came, I felt build up inside me the strangest expectation. I do not know why I experienced such a sensation for to be in a house of such standing was not a new experience for me. Yet this expectation was deflated to some degree as the servant opened the door and I saw standing there at the virginal, where I had imagined a pretty young lady might be, Monsieur Huygens himself. He turned around, a little embarrassed, wearing an expression of boyish knowingness, which betrayed nevertheless a certain effeminacy.

'A new piece I have acquired. I am not happy with my rendition, however—' he began.

I stood transfixed by the instrument. It was not the first time I had seen a virginal, but it suited the space and design of this Dutch interior in a manner that appealed beyond my ability to explain. Certainly, its position in the room close to a window, with the angled light of that time of day, along with double, competing shadows that nestled slightly to the right of the legs and the lid, imparted a sense of *déjà vu.*

'I cannot fault your playing,' I replied, marvelling at the curious seahorse shapes on either side of, as well as above, the keyboard.

'Well, do not tell it abroad. Rumours will start that I have nothing better to do.'

'But Mijn Heer Huygens, if I had the smallest portion of your renowned taste and talents . . .'

'And I the smallest of your discoveries.' He paused, and, as if to curtail the spiral of compliments, said, archly, 'We should combine our knowledge.'

I did not think anything of this comment at the time, though perhaps I could be excused this laxity, given my absorption in my particular surroundings; I was still engaged in translating the Latin inscription on the lid of the instrument when he motioned me towards the next room, where we sat down to dine.

The servant now reappeared and filled our glasses.

'So your departure has been delayed?' Monsieur Huygens asked, though I did not know from where he might have gleaned this knowledge.

'I wish it could be postponed indefinitely. I have, alas, not been successful in my attempt to investigate the work of Mijn Heer Vermeer, whom you recommended so highly.'

'How so?'

'He had no pictures to show. It was only at the home of a nearby tradesman that I was fortunate to see a piece by him of a lute player.' I could not suppress a nervous laugh. It seemed ridiculous to me that I had been reduced to visiting a common baker in search of art.

'Yes, I know the work of which you speak.'

'And Mijn Heer van Ruijven was not in Delft.' I paused, hoping he would assist me, but he persisted in his reticence. 'Would you know when he returns? Perhaps I could pay another visit during my travels around Holland? I could apprise you of my itinerary . . .'

Monsieur Huygens showed here the aspect of concern, but his was an expression that I have seen so often on the faces of the wealthy. It said, I am too engaged myself to care for such matters.

'What you report,' he said, 'is most unfortunate. I have myself experienced Mijn Heer Vermeer's perplexing modesty. But he cannot hide long from such curious souls as we.'

I was encouraged by this call to unity, but I found the insistent look given me by the Count of Zulcon, or however the esteemed Monsieur Huygens chooses to call himself, unsettling.

'I am perhaps not well informed about Mijn Heer Vermeer's exact standing in Delft. I was not as impressed by his lute player as I had been led to expect,' I continued.

'Monsieur de Monconys, you astound me in some respects.'

'I am not certain what you mean.'

'You are so well travelled, so learned, yet you cannot judge the importance of a gentleman such as Mijn Heer Vermeer.'

How could I explain to *this* man the confounding nature of his country without insulting him? I knew and understood Spain, Portugal, Italy, and Egypt more than I did these small towns where swans could lay their eggs beside canals without fear of disturbance.

'It might avail you to know that he is currently headman of St Luke's Guild, a post of some responsibility. And a member of the local militia.'

The last parcel of knowledge he imparted with some distinct pride, I sensed.

'I should like to know more of his working methods,' I continued in another vein, as I felt my ignorance of Dutch civic life might lead me to cause offence.

'His methods?'

'I had at least the little fortune to see the initial stages of a new piece. I must say that it fascinates me as if I had already known it before the first viewing.'

Monsieur Huygens relinquished the sternness that had momentarily taken over his voice, his interest palpably piqued.

'And this piece, can you describe it?'

'I can only recall some tiles, a mirror, some windows, some Spanish leather chairs, and a virginal such as you . . .'

'Ah, he has been speaking of such a perspective as this. But, in truth, it sounds like many a picture he has already executed. I find that it is not so much the content as the manner of his pieces that fascinates.'

He said these words with a display of great satisfaction, as if he thought he had succeeded in veiling his true excitement.

'You commissioned the work?'

'No, *I* did not commission it.'

From the accent that he placed on this one word, as if he would deny being identified as the patron of the work in question, I expected more information to follow, an elucidation of a sense of regret, perhaps, but, instead, Monsieur Huygens rose, saying, 'Will you not come and see some of the wonderful instruments my son has acquired? His achievements already surpass what I had hoped for. He is presently in London, you know.'

So we climbed the narrow stairs to a well-appointed room, which had a most splendid view of the skies. In the room, I noticed a large map hung as you would a picture on a wall. In addition to this, a golden, metal-plated disc caught the light of our candelabra as we moved about. I recognised it for an astrolabe. Monsieur Huygens proceeded to take the device onto the balcony and adjust it so that he could align it with the stars. His excitement was so evident that I had no desire to spoil it by telling him that I was already familiar with such instruments.

'Was it from here that your son discovered the rings of Saturn?' I said, unable to hold back this knowledge any longer.

'You are well informed, Monsieur de Monconys. I suspect that, like Mijn Heer Vermeer, you keep much to yourself.'

'But such knowledge should be shared, surely?'

'Yes, indeed. I have no right to joke with you.'

'Well, I am most honoured by what you have shared with me tonight. I hope that I will finally appreciate what it is in Mijn Heer Vermeer's work that I have not been sensitive to till now.'

'Of that I am certain.'

On my return to the Duke's residence that evening, I was struck by the distance that he appeared to maintain. He had little to report and fewer demands of me than was his custom. Over supper he finally told me his thoughts.

'Monsieur de Monconys, I am a man who cares little for the humdrum tasks of life. On occasion we wander away from them. I too, though we must always return. And I see that your interests take you far from this area at the present moment. I see in you some impatience, and I shall not have it so. I put it to you, therefore, that if there is a certain matter you wish to complete before our departure, then I am happy to grant you the time necessary.'

I was astonished beyond measure. I had known the Duke for a man possessed of an acute judgement of his fellows, but not one to bend to the whims of a companion such as myself. I told him that I was most grateful for his indulgence, and let it be implied that this was doubly so, since I did not dare to specify the cause of my growing unease, and was grateful that this was not demanded of me.

'There is indeed a small matter, in Delft, which I should like further to investigate.'

'How much time do you require?'

'A week, perhaps a few days more,' I replied tentatively.

'Then I shall grant you ten days.'

I took my leave immediately, went to my desk and wrote letters to Monsieur Borry and Monsieur van Ruijven requesting an audience. As soon as I had dispatched these to Delft, my thoughts turned to the unfortunate Monsieur Borry and whether I should not enquire after his welfare.

My carriage arrived as another, familiar to me as that of Monsieur Huygens, was driving away. I should not have been surprised at the presence of that gentleman at Monsieur Borry's house, except for the lateness of the hour.

And indeed, it was only after some insistent ringing of the bell that Monsieur Borry came to the door. He stood in his nightgown holding a candle within a narrow area, which I felt he would be reluctant to widen.

'Monsieur de Monconys! I do not recommend you visit here now.'

'But Monsieur Borry, what is wrong? Can I not help you?'

'Look after yourself, Monsieur de Monconys. I can only tell you that. Do not worry about me. You have been very kind. Please take your leave.'

'But was that not Monsieur . . . ?'

He had closed the door before I could finish, though there was no doubt he knew what I had intended to say.

Returning to my carriage, I was taken by a sharp pain in my side, of a kind I had felt more and more frequently of late. I told myself that my body was perhaps responding in sympathy with the strange behaviour of my countryman.

Later the next day I received a message from Monsieur van Ruijven brought to me by a young man wearing a fine, gold-embroidered jacket. I had at first taken him to be a soldier of some kind, dressed as he was like some messenger out of a picture by Terborch, but his manner in no way supported this prejudice. I read the message while he waited.

*To the esteemed Monsieur de Monconys,*

*I regret that I could not meet you on the occasion of your recent visit to Delft. However, I believe that we may have matters to discuss which might be of benefit to us both and, indeed, to Mijn Heer Vermeer, with whom I enjoy a particular relationship and in whose welfare I take an exceptional interest.*

*I think I do not exaggerate when I inform you that I am offering you an opportunity such as few people have experienced.*

*I await your arrival with pleasure.*

*Pieter Claesz. van Ruijven*

The messenger remained impassive. Even Dutch people of the lowest rank, it was apparent to me, distinguished themselves with good breeding. Too often I had known my own servants in France to show mocking insolence at the slightest opportunity. Was it my natural naïveté that occasioned such behaviour?

'Tell your master I shall be in Delft by midday.'

He showed a look of surprise, bowed, and left.

The journey by towing barge, which lasted one hour, afforded me time to consider. Why did this Monsieur van Ruijven now wish to see me? Was I to be granted a private viewing in the hope that I should buy a piece of art? In that event I was afraid that I might disappoint him. Was there perhaps some connection with Monsieur Borry and his chemicals?

I gazed at the flatness of the landscape. Only the spires of the churches could resist the enormity of the sky. Once more I observed in the fields some bulls sleeping in the shade of an oak, a maid milking a cow, solitary figures in meadows all to themselves, small barges carrying goods. Yet the peacefulness of the view began to oppress me. Was I sick?

I arrived before midday with time to visit the Nieuwe Kerk once more, which I had since my last visit seen represented on some intriguing canvases. I wanted to know if my memory had not deceived me in respect of certain small details.

It was not my memory that had fooled me, I now saw.

I looked first down the nave, noticing a group of black-caped burghers gathered around William the Silent's tomb. From there my attention moved to the floor. I was confirmed in my speculation. I had remembered black-and-white tiles, yet I was confronted with yellow-brown flagstones. To my left, I saw a gravedigger working in the ground. He had interrupted his work to stare at me. At my feet was a small mound of earth, and very near to these, a dog was urinating against a pillar. When I met his gaze again, the man looked away and went about his task once more.

As I left, I noticed an artist working at his easel. I glanced at the bare design of his picture, which, it occurred to me, diverged greatly from the view I could see. I would have stayed to ask him some questions, but I was unwell. I felt that pain once more in my stomach; I was in need of a place of privacy.

The humiliation continued as I looked for a place to relieve myself. I had no choice but to enter a tavern, and walked into a soldier as he was leaving. I found the impact with his cuirass, polished and elegant as it may have been, most painful. The expression on the soldier's face, along with those of his companions, was far from apologetic. It seems that they had recognised me for what

I was, a representative of France, and they had no care for my status.

They left, laughing, the tips of their low-swung swords striking my outstretched feet as they went. Finally, I was helped to my feet by a maid.

She showed no embarrassment as she pointed to the courtyard, where I found a cabin that contained a large chamber pot.

I think the same maid noticed my indisposition as I returned to the tavern, because she brought me a strange milk-like concoction, which eased the discomfort in my stomach noticeably. I sat in a quiet corner and drank it down, becoming only gradually aware that the atmosphere I had disturbed was returning. Attention had turned away from me, and I was able to recognise a very different tavern from that managed by Monsieur Vermeer's mother.

I was now certainly late for Monsieur van Ruijven, but felt much better. I would at least arrive there in a state in which I could appreciate the favour that was being done for me.

I had thought myself familiar with the topography of this city, its architecture of exterior and interior. Yet I found, even on my short walk to Van Ruijven's place, that I still did not have the measure of this culture. And I was overcome by a sensation I had rarely admitted to and which I am passing on to you, my dear Ferdinand, for the first time. In certain circumstances, often during my travels, I have experienced this sensation of being far from my home, as if I am a child who has strayed, whilst my father comes in vociferous pursuit. At times, I am both pushed forward into the centre of my own point of vision and immensely distant from the subject of my view. Such an introduction may seem grandiloquent, but the feeling that I have described will, I believe, serve to show how I was prepared, in spite of myself, for a revelation.

Monsieur van Ruijven's residence was, contrary to my expectations, not grand in style, but, rather, precise and detailed. While this Monsieur van Ruijven was wealthy in a manner that went beyond ostentation, his residence showed a precision, a sense of orderliness and selection in his tastes that I had not encountered elsewhere in Holland.

After seeing off his servant, he devoted himself to me. He was frail to look at, his face bony, and his features recalled the look of certain kinds of French aristocrat. We sat for some time before a fire, the only interruptions being those of the maid, who trundled occasionally past with her metal pail and mop. I found these excursions somewhat disturbing, though Monsieur van Ruijven only seemed to find amusement in my discomfiture.

When many cordial remarks were behind us, we began to speak of the matter at hand.

'It was Mijn Heer Vermeer who recommended you to me?' Monsieur van Ruijven said finally.

'Yes, though he said no more than that,' I replied.

'How many pictures have you seen?'

'Of Mijn Heer Vermeer's?' I said, uncertain.

He nodded, as if it were self-evident.

'Only two. A certain lute player at the home of a baker, then a recently begun piece, I would say a music lesson.'

Monsieur van Ruijven lowered his head into his outheld hands, as if in a gesture of pious thankfulness.

'You have seen little, then.'

I was tantalised by these words, yet hardly certain if this recommended me to him or made me a disappointment.

'You have chosen a strange time to come to Delft.'

Again, there was a pause, which I was unable to fill.

'It is my estimation that you know nothing of Mijn Heer Vermeer's state of mind. I have not invited you here as a collector. I have no intention of parting with my own acquisitions. I would simply like to make your journey as worthwhile as possible, in a way that he might be unable to.'

'But is it not true that Monsieur Vermeer is presently a headman of the Guild, that he is required to express considered opinions on all aspects of his art and trade?'

'I see that you have been informed of Mijn Heer Vermeer's importance and, indeed, of his performance of civic functions. However, there are those of us who take an interest in helping to direct a talent such as his to the greater good.'

'The greater good?'

Monsieur van Ruijven did not meet my eye, but scratched the back of one hand, which I noticed was a little purple.

'These are but idle words. First I should like to show you the things of which we really speak.' As we stood, he added, 'You do not have to hurry back, I trust?'


If there is such a thing as a dark paradise then I think I encountered it that day.


The pictures were disposed about the house as if they might indicate someone's soul, without revealing the mind or the person. And yet this was most certainly, most worryingly, an unusual display, as there was another's, a collector's, mind at work. In an antechamber, I passed a large picture of Jesus with Martha and Mary, then a mythical piece, of Diana, identifiable as such from her crown, though it seemed the piece was set at dawn or during twilight rather than night. Another large piece showed a scene so familiar from the Dutch masters, a brothel scene to be sure, of a brightly-clad soldier passing a coin into the hand of a rosy-cheeked, buxom maid. This work was entirely a strange gathering together of figures in a place of whose dimensions I could not be certain, though in the bare light permitted by the corridor, the yellows and reds were so bright as to make me fear my own clothes might be dyed if I wandered too close.

Another, smaller, room showed a view that I at first took for a window, from which I could see the city of Delft. Yet I knew it could not be so, this orange, sandy shore, the grey-green water of the harbour, these rust-red roofs that I thought I might touch.

I was drawn on by the sight of a seated maid, it seemed to me, sleeping at a table in a room beyond this, her head gently resting on her hand. I should not intrude on her, was my first thought, though I noticed it was no real maid but once more a painted image of one. Yet I found myself gazing on her as if I were spying on just such a living creature.

I walked into the largest room of all, in which I saw perhaps fifteen pieces collected together. A woman in a yellow jacket with black-trimmed sleeves and a black dress stood solemnly at a window with her letter; another woman in a large blue jacket was similarly engaged, with a map for background. In fact, all around me were young women, as if gathered for a display of their private preoccupations, whether engaged in the most mundane or more worldly activities.

I heard voices, the sound of a lute, whispers, the pouring of liquids, the rustle of paper, the sound of earthenware alighting on carpet, laughter, gentle coaxing and cajolery. I felt intoxicated by this indulgence of my senses and yet anxious, realising suddenly that I was alone, save perhaps for the maid. Yet I was anxious for yet another reason. How was it possible that all these pictures here, in one place, were the possession of one person?

Nevertheless, I stayed, and I was not disturbed.

To be sure, there were other scenes, of companionship, where gentlemen importuned ladies, drank wine, or accompanied them at music, and there was a most delightful picture of a little street where the inhabitants of a house went about their work and play oblivious of the intricate detail of texture all around them. Yet it was perhaps the solitary scenes of women that arrested me most.

Of course, I had forgotten my host, and only now did I ask myself where he might be. It proved an unnecessary concern. As I continued on, through rooms that implied a deeper depth to the house than could possibly be, I heard not only Monsieur van Ruijven's, but another's, familiar voice.

It was an uncommon sight to see Monsieur Vermeer formally dressed. He was leaning against a large marble mantelpiece surmounted by a mirror. His long, black coat, which let his voluminous shirtsleeves show, his cane, and his white sash—these all cast my previous impression of the man in another light.

Monsieur van Ruijven greeted me as if I had been gone for most of the day.

'Ah, Monsieur de Monconys, please take a chair.'

I could not but notice how my host's face carried a note of concern when he saw me. I became aware of my own expression in the mirror, of a face much travelled in life, to be sure, but which now betrayed the experience of another journey. And this face was at the centre of a trio of worthy gentlemen, with Monsieur van Ruijven to its left, and Monsieur Vermeer to its right, as if life were seeking to compose itself to the design of one of Monsieur Vermeer's own pictures.

This happy symmetry disappeared as soon as I sat down, following which the two gentlemen joined me by taking to their respective chairs.

'I am honoured once more, gentlemen,' I said, uncertain what was expected of me.

'I think that your bearing betrays a great satisfaction with the work of Mijn Heer Vermeer. I hope I am not wrong in supposing this to be the case,' Monsieur van Ruijven replied.

'Oh, no, most assuredly not. I am fascinated by what I have seen. Although perhaps troubled too.'

'Troubled?' Monsieur van Ruijven asked.

'To see so many of Mijn Heer Vermeer's works in one place. How, if I may ask, will Mijn Heer Vermeer's name travel abroad with so many pictures concentrated here?'

'Well, that is for Mijn Heer Vermeer to decide and posterity to answer,' Monsieur van Ruijven said, with an air of finality.

It seemed that Monsieur Vermeer would not participate at all in this conversation unless stimulated to.

'But I do not understand, Mijn Heer Vermeer,' I said, 'how you can achieve such results as these. You must have a special recipe to gain such effects.' I think I should have been afraid of showing my boyish enthusiasm too openly, of being mocked, but I could not hold myself back.

Monsieur van Ruijven scratched his beard, while Monsieur Vermeer sat back in his chair.

'It is a vexed question,' Monsieur van Ruijven interrupted, to my frustration, and continued, 'If you will permit me to ask: Does a poet reveal the means by which he comes to a certain rhythm and metre, or, indeed, a maker of fortifications explain his strategies to the enemy?'

This unfortunate analogy disquieted me.

'The enemy?' I questioned. 'I cannot imagine what enemies we should be speaking of, in the world of art.'

'Indeed,' Monsieur van Ruijven pursued, 'we are not speaking of simple artistic rivalry or of national considerations, but of truth, of philosophy, in short, of *technique*.'

'You astonish me,' I said, 'for that is all that interests me here.'

'Yes, but you are perhaps not aware that such things need to be protected.'

'Protected? Protected from what?' I said, hoping that my exasperation would not be interpreted as aggression. I had to question my own faculties of understanding. Were we still speaking of painting, or military secrets?

'Monsieur de Monconys,' Monsieur van Ruijven said, drawing in a deep breath, as if for some revelation, 'you have come here to Delft at a most intriguing and difficult time. We have, from the very beginning, been uncertain as to your motivation for this visit.'

While Monsieur van Ruijven spoke these words, I sensed Monsieur Vermeer's blue-eyed gaze on me, and began to entertain deep thoughts that I might have made some terrible mistake. Perhaps war had been declared between our countries, perhaps there was some plot. I thought of the assassination of William the Silent in Delft by one of my own faith almost a century before, and, looking into the eyes of these two gentlemen, who I had taken for so long as men concerned with little more than art and its trade, saw myself as perhaps the target of their opprobrium.

'To wit, in some days' time there will be a conclave here, of the kind rarely seen before, which will bring together men of such standing as to amaze you. If we did not believe your presence to be of the most genuine and innocent kind, we would not have told you this much. I am taking a risk in inviting you, but your participation could be beneficial.'

'What, may I ask, is the nature of this conclave?'

'I think you should ask Monsieur Vermeer. You will take your leave with him now.'

I felt that Monsieur Vermeer's look did not quite display trust in me despite our host's words; I noticed how his large hands played nervously in his pockets.

When we were outside, however, his disposition changed markedly. I had expected to walk with him towards the Great Market, but he took my arm to direct me to the south of the town. We soon reached the Rotterdam Gate and passed from there over the Kolk to another street.

We now stood before a view that seemed familiar, though my brief memory questioned the reality of what I saw. Most certainly, I recognised this view from the canvas I had seen in Monsieur van Ruijven's collection. But my heart sank a little as I acknowledged differences between the picture and the source of inspiration for it. The port was busy, and I sensed in the man standing beside me a certain irritation. It seemed, as I recalled, that the painter had brought elements, such as the towers of the Oude and Nieuwe Kerken closer together than was my privilege here to witness. It was as if the actual view, in being rendered on a canvas, had, after drying, contracted into a sharper and more intense image. I could not but remark on this.

'I am not certain which to prefer, Monsieur Vermeer, the original picture or its counterfeit.' Even as I said this, however, the term 'counterfeit' did not sound correct.

'If you desire the original, do not seek it in the picture, Monsieur,' he replied, startling me with the first words of substance he had uttered since my visit to his patron.

'Then can we not speak of the picture as being *truer*?' I speculated.

'There are some who would, as you will find at the conclave, replace this truer reality with its very likeness,' he said, demonstrating, I thought, some aggressiveness.

'Oh? How would that be possible?' I said disingenuously. It was impossible to put from my mind that unearthly image Borry had shown me.

'You will see, soon enough,' he said with seeming finality, then added, 'You are familiar with the camera obscura box?'

I nodded, and I expected him to enthuse about this exciting device, but he turned thoughtful and inward, a state I was reluctant to disturb. I followed him back along the Oude Delft, where we stopped in front of a house.

'Pieter de Hooch lived here,' he said.

'De Hooch?' I marvelled. 'Where is he now?'

'He lives in Amsterdam. I have heard he is successful.'

'Fabritius too lived near here?'

'Fabritius died an untimely death.'

'Oh?'

'You do not know?'

'No.'

'The powder explosion. You hadn't heard of it?'

I shrugged my shoulders, a little embarrassed. I knew more about the Leiden painters, such as Dou and Van Mieris, who, it seemed to me, were held in greater respect and enjoyed more financial security than their Delft counterparts.

'I sometimes think that there are dark forces at work in this town,' he continued.

'Dark forces?'

'Not supernatural, but something against all of us.'

'But what could these forces be? If I may say, there is no evidence of this in what you paint.'

'Let us discuss these matters in my painting room.'

I was most pleased at the invitation, thankful that I had had no need to provoke it. During this return trip I was left further tantalised when Monsieur Vermeer indicated, almost casually, the house of Anthony van Leeuwenhoek, a maker of lenses, responsible for much progress with the first microscopes. I felt overwhelmed by the vast and timely concordance of so much talent and discovery in such a small town as this, and the very little time I would have to investigate it further.

He sat deep in his chair, arms resting on its sides, against the muted light of the tinted window, wearing a lustrous green robe far too valuable to be used while he painted. I must admit, I felt a little cheated, afraid I would be denied a practical demonstration of his work. Instead, this master of light and colour, I saw, intended to paint a picture of his world in words.

'My parents gave me the kind of attention which did not prepare me for life. Even my sister is guilty in that respect. She treated me as special, to her own detriment. So much attention pushed me inward; it made me retreat, made me sensitive, made me distrustful.'

I had not expected words of this nature to come from this man; I had gone from feeling indifferent towards him to craving direct contact with him.

'Naturally, I was grateful for the training I was given,' he went on, 'and for the discoveries made by so many of my fellow townsmen. I have not begrudged them their relative success, whereas, because of the course my life has taken, I have been compelled to compromise.'

I must have looked quizzical because he added, 'My wife's mother, the Catholic faith, I embraced it. Just as it has helped me in certain ways, it has hindered in others.'

'Oh?' I queried.

'Just look around at the number of my offspring already. And my children, should they even desire them, are barred from certain civic positions. And yet, I cannot deny that Catharina's mother has brought me into contact with patrons of a higher class and even that she has a little money saved, some land . . .

'But I am aware that progress is slow. I have seen things. The barbarity of war, witchcraft, all kinds of summary punishment. Even life cut down as it left the mother's womb, my Catharina's. I have also seen a great talent destroyed.'

'Fabritius?' I said.

His features seemed to retreat into the very shadows they projected, and I had the sensation that our relative positions were changing, though we were both still seated, as if his words were describing a chaconne to which I was dancing, as if he, as the object of my view and subject to the rules of parallax, seemed to be moving too.

'He died before his time. He would have been at the centre of this conclave had he lived.'

He chuckled fondly, as if contemplating the mischievousness of a loved friend. Then he added, 'I sometimes think he has organised the whole thing.'

'Did he teach you?'

'Not formally. He was my mentor for a while, but I did not paint in his presence.'

'Who was your teacher?'

'My early teachers were Bramer and Van Loo, both fine men. Then there was De Hooch, Terborch . . .'

'Terborch?'

'For a time.'

'He is famous indeed.'

'Indeed, but he is not half the master he should be. And his reputation sullies his achievement.'

'And you, what is the foundation of your art? What is your comfort while you await people's slow opinions?'

'I have my duties in the Guild. From time to time my opinion is asked.'

'Pupils?'

'None.'

'You do everything?'

'I have to.'

He looked at me as if to say this was evident.

'For myself. It's the only way to be certain of the result.'

'I would love to see your present labours brought to perfection.'

'You shall, and perhaps something more. You can stay tonight?'

'Yes, but . . .'

'You may stay in the inn. There is a room free.'

I was delighted by this news. I believe I could not have hoped for a more favourable circumstance.

'Besides,' he continued, 'the conclave is tomorrow, and you might help me, I dare to presume.'

\* \* \*

I retired happy in the knowledge that I had been shown the most unexpected trust by these gentlemen. My only anxiety was for events to proceed as quickly as possible, not because the Duke had demanded it, for indeed he had given me time in generous measure, but to satisfy my own curiosity.

I was given the room next to Monsieur Vermeer's painting room, which I considered an honour. Outside, I heard the town crier; within, the mildly remonstrating voices of the inn's last customers. This apart, there was nothing to disturb me of thoughts of your dear mother and our country, and of the forthcoming journey I would make. Yet I was aware that, as exciting as the rest of my travels would surely prove to be, I could not enter into them wholeheartedly until I knew what was taking place in this beguiling town.

I fell into a deep sleep and dreamt that I was walking around a town foreign to me, searching for something to which I could not put a name. I entered many patrician houses, where I was shown various pictures and beautiful pieces of furniture. From a window I saw what seemed to be a ship sailing through a street just behind the next row of houses, its enormous white sails flapping serenely, yet completely silent. Then I was in an old craftsman's workshop, looking into a mirror, but I was woken by the sound of feet outside my door. I saw under it a strip of light that moved on to the painting room where it reappeared most surprisingly in the centre of the adjacent wall as if another door indeed connected my host's workroom to my room. Some minutes later, I heard the sound of another person's feet approaching, the soft tapping against my neighbour's door, and the sound of a woman calling the name of Johannes. But he did not reply.

'Johannes, come to bed,' she pursued, as if to a child. 'I am sorry.'

She did not stay long; the silence from within the room had given way to that of a person within going about a most determined task.

I was fully awake, and, finding the need to relieve myself, felt I should exercise discretion in my use of the bowl beneath my bed.

The next morning I was woken by the sound of Monsieur Vermeer moving about his room. Had he been working all night, by candle?

My curiosity would not allow me any longer to keep a distance. Putting my eye to the keyhole to what I now saw was indeed a door to his workroom, I was a little confused to see nothing except triangles of clear morning light filling the room, the virginal to my right, the viola da gamba straight ahead, the covered table close to me on the left, in fact all the objects I had seen before. The canvas and easel I could not see, nor Monsieur Vermeer himself, though I could hear his occasional cough or sigh. Then I realised. The virginal. There was now in Monsieur Vermeer's workroom an instrument such as I had seen only on his canvas and at Monsieur Huygens' home, and I had viewed it as if I was already accustomed to seeing it in this house, when in fact it was the first time. It must have been brought in that very morning.

The sound of footsteps approaching my door made me pull up abruptly.

The painter's mother found me standing aimlessly in the centre of the room with my hands joined behind my back. If my occupation appeared eccentric to her, she did not show it, but merely enquired whether I had slept well and then she invited me to breakfast. As I prepared myself, I heard her call her son and he in turn expressed his annoyance at this interruption, though I could not know the exact meaning of his words.

During breakfast Monsieur Vermeer made no reference to the nocturnal altercation with his wife, but excused himself briefly to visit her when he had eaten.

On his return, he kept me waiting no longer and we went up to his painting room.

'I am under some pressure,' he said, as we went in.

I was aware of a change in the room. It was very clear that perhaps a third of the room had disappeared behind a wooden partition, though I could not guess to what purpose.

'I hope I didn't disturb you in the night,' he said in explanation.

My discomfiture must have been in evidence as I acknowledged his apology. Would he guess that such a man as I would stoop to spying through a hole to learn of his methods? Would he accept such a motivation, indeed?

But it seemed he was expecting me to make a connection between his activities of the previous evening and the altered dimensions of the room. I now understood that there must be a connection, but I still could not understand what exactly.

He continued to look from me to the wooden partition and back again. I followed the direction of his gaze on each occasion, but I could not see what he was indicating. However, eventually I saw something shining in the middle of the partition, a small glassy substance set into the wood at eye-level. He realised I had found it.

'Now, come closer,' he said.

For perhaps the first time, I felt as if Monsieur Vermeer, usually so solemn, was taking a mischievous pleasure in prolonging the revelation of this mystery.

As I studied the hole filled with glass, he explained, 'It is a lens, newly developed by Van Leeuwenhoek.'

I nodded, whereupon he reached out for a handle that had been painted over so as to fool the eye of its presence, as indeed had been the door itself.

He entered, and from the dark, he beckoned me in.

We were in darkness, yet the light that I saw, conveyed along a funnel through the air, was a bold circular disc brighter than the day itself from which we had just retreated.

It was a surface of another kind, not moving, to be sure, yet containing minute motion as is only seen in the air around us. I felt as if I was pressed up against a large object and could not identify the thing all the while. This sensation was followed by the realisation that I was looking at different areas of flat, concentrated colours that became ever stronger. And here I started at a sudden darkening, as if, as if, could it be, a cloud were passing over this view?

'I think, I think I know what I am seeing, Mijn Heer Vermeer, but this cannot be possible.'

The cloud, if such it was, had passed, and the intense brightness of colour returned. And with it, forms that I could now identify.

Though I was facing away from these objects, I could see, perhaps even more clearly than if they were before me, a virginal, a Spanish leather chair, a table covered with a carpet, a mirror, a viola da gamba, and, perhaps most impressively, two bays of tinted windows, from which undeniably the true source of what I was seeing issued. Yet such was, and still is, my excitement at what I saw at that moment, my dear Ferdinand, that I almost forget to mention that all of this sight was inverted. The mirror, virginal, chair, and windows, all these occupied the lower half of the bright circle, whilst the carpet, table and viola da gamba inhabited the upper part, 'It is your picture, sir.'

He gave out a short, ironic laugh.

'It is more than my picture, Monsieur. It is the room outside this one.'

'One it is your intention to counterfeit in that manner peculiar to you.'

'Your words are well chosen, though I do not think that you know how true they are.'

'I am an amateur when it comes to such matters.'

Before he could retort in kind, we heard a knock on the door to the room, which was to the side of our little partition.

'But she is too early,' Monsieur Vermeer said under his breath. More particularly to me, he said, 'Do not speak.'

We waited and listened as someone entered.

'Mijn Heer Vermeer?' The voice was a little inelegant, but it was nevertheless possessed of an inquiring intelligence. I thought I heard the brush of long, heavy material along the tiled floor as she walked alongside the partition and entered the room.

'Mijn Heer Vermeer? Mijn Heer Vermeer, I am ready.'

The master sensed my intention to reply and stayed me with his hand.

'Wait. Look,' he whispered.

She was standing closer to the wooden partition than to the back wall against which I now noticed were composed a series of rectangles which conveyed to me, in their unusual asymmetry, a harmonious message, so that it was possible to give her features due consideration. She was a naturally pale young woman with cheeks which had been painstakingly, albeit incongruously, rouged, but with eyes set slightly back with the effect that her character stood out all the more. Those eyes were searching, intelligent ones. Did she already know of the painter's secret chamber? As I thought about this, I heard Monsieur Vermeer stifle his obvious amusement.

'But . . . she is the most sweet thing . . . I think I could love her as my own daughter,' he continued.

'Master?' she called out again, now walking away and moving to the right where was situated the connecting door to my room. As she did so, she seemed to move with the elegance of one assisted by some other power. I hesitate to say that of a spirit because I abhor such superstition—and I thought that her body left behind it the faintest of contours, of a grey-blue tone, in the space it had just vacated, somewhat as the eye retains the outline of the sun after one has had the good sense to look away. Curiously, at the same time, the distance she passed into was to my eyes exaggerated by our special view of the scene. As she passed from the door to look into the mirror above the virginal, I thought rather unreasonably that she had seen us.

As if sensing the same, he said, 'We must finally reveal our little secret, I think,' and pushed the door open. The light flooded in, so that I could see but poorly for a while. The view that I saw now struck me as pretty, to be sure, but it was poor in comparison to what I remembered from inside that small room.

The light was harsher, the brighter colours seemed obstinately, in almost a vulgar way, to attach themselves to their surfaces in comparison with their darker companions. The room itself seemed vertiginously small by comparison. It was only when I concentrated fully on the face of the woman before me that my disappointment stopped.

'I am sorry. You are shocked,' he said to her. 'This

is Monsieur de Monconys. He has travelled from France to view our fair town of Delft.'

I did not wish to contradict Monsieur Vermeer on the finer points of my reason for coming here, especially as it was now obvious to me that I was dealing with the painter's model, and not, as I had first thought, his wife, to whom she bore a marked resemblance.

'But I am forgetting,' he said to me suddenly. 'I had arranged for her to come this morning. I could send word to delay him, but it is essential I work now while the light is as it is.'

'I do not want to disturb you in any way.'

'I think you should stay . . . Van Ruijven can wait a day. Besides, your presence has inspired me, and I believe I know what will interest you even more . . . I can show you how it works. Then we can eat in my . . . well, my mother-in-law's house. Besides, there is still a matter of some gravity of which I must speak to you. Maritje here will be assisting me in the project too.'

I thought he might be speaking of the conclave but I could not guess at the nature of the project.

'Maritje, I shall only need you for some minutes, as it turns out. Stand by the virginal, will you.'

She went over to the instrument, but stood a little aimlessly beside it, I thought, only then to drift towards the window, from which she seemed to gaze engrossed, rapt.

From the corner of the room Monsieur Vermeer produced the canvas I had seen on my first visit to the studio, and I noticed some changes in the general design of the picture. The regularity of the diamond-like tiles, which seemed to reach down at the viewer and involve him all the more in the space of the picture, struck me in particular. As I have said before, they were not the tiles I saw before me in the studio; they were larger, and coloured in black and white.

'I cannot explain my feeling in this matter,' I stumbled out awkwardly, 'but I would say that the construction of the tiles and the use of the dark chamber have imparted something most essential to this picture that I have not seen before . . .'

'I am not happy with the results, but there has been progress in the design, to be sure,' he said almost apologetically, then looked over at Maritje.

'I am sorry, Maritje. I shall not need you today after all, though I shall pay you nevertheless. These things take time, Maritje. Perhaps the light will be better tomorrow. Convey my apologies to Mijn Heer van Ruijven.'

He turned to me as if I deserved an explanation. It was as if he trusted me already so much.

'She is the charge of my patron Van Ruijven and he would have her included in this picture. But it was hardly my original idea.'

'Indeed?'

'Which was a portrait of Catharina and myself. What is more, he would have it soon. For what reason, it is not my place or desire to ask.'

When she had gone, he buried his head in one hand as if he were afflicted by a sudden head pain, saying, 'In any case, I should have started with the mirror, then . . . But let me show you something.'

He took a canvas the exact size of the half-completed one that stood on the easel, and placed it on a large board on his bench. Then he took a small pin and placed it in the exact centre of the canvas, at a point where in the original picture the elbow of the woman standing at the virginal could be found. He then drew a horizontal line through this point, a little over halfway up the canvas, right across the canvas and beyond the edges on both sides. He took two nails and tapped one into the board along this horizon line at the extreme edge, and another on the opposite side.

He then took a piece of string that he attached to the nail on the left of the canvas. I noticed a small cloud of chalk puff out from it when he snapped it so that it left a light diagonal line on the surface of the canvas. He did the same twice more; so that I could now see light cone-like shapes proceeding up towards the distant left point. But he was not finished. He now took the string, and attaching it to the nail on the right, pulled this down across the canvas so that it intersected the chalk lines already made. He repeated this action on the right side, then again, at certain regular angles on either side, so that I now saw as if by magic a very convincing tile construction. Lastly, he joined the string to the centre pin and made this intersect the tiles at regular intervals to create an effect that added a most convincing sense of depth to the illustration.

Before I could praise this ingenious artifice, he said, 'But I am not satisfied here. The tiles at the bottom are not as the eye would see them.'

'Why do you not lower the eye-point?'

'I have given that some thought, but,' he laughed nervously, 'then I could not have the composition, the distance I need here.'

I directed his attention to the canvas on the easel and for a short time, as he turned from the indeterminate features of a face reflected in the mirror in that picture, to where Maritje had stood by the window, I could see that he was not happy.

'The time, in any case, will not suffice,' he said. "I must tell you about the conclave. And it is a matter that

I need to discuss . . . away from this. Come, we shall have lunch at my mother-in-law's house.'

I must admit that I entered Monsieur Vermeer's 'mother-in-law's house' with some trepidation, if only because he had described as such the place where I had the day before visited so briefly and encountered the handsome wife of this man. I think I had sensed in her bearing some guardedness, beneath which a kindly disposition lodged. So how would her mother-in-law, whose house it was, and whose name I did not yet know, regard me—both a stranger and a foreigner in this state of feverish excitement, to which I had been brought by what I had seen that morning?

As we crossed the square, the pungent smell of fish from the market and the aroma of baked bread mixing with my thoughts, Monsieur Vermeer said, 'Maria Thins appears a stern woman, but I owe her much. She showed trust in me where others of her standing might have deferred to caution. She is a woman treated ill by her husband and son, a circumstance from which she recovered well, as you will soon see.'

We were there within one minute, whereupon three small Vermeers, for such I took them to be, streamed out of the door on our entering. Monsieur Vermeer smiled amusement but did not seem overly concerned with their clamour. He looked at me as if to say: Life goes on.

This time, indeed, we were met by Catharina's mother. I understood immediately what Monsieur Vermeer had tried to communicate to me. In her appearance she reminded me of a patrician's wife, a living portrait such as many I had seen in Rembrandt van Rijn's work.

'The celebrated visitor from France,' she said, as we stood in the hallway. 'I hope that if you have come to buy some of my son-in-law's pictures, you will do them justice.'

'Madam, I do not think that I can take any such purchase for granted.'

'Monsieur de Monconys' principal reason for visiting was the *church*, mother,' Monsieur Vermeer mediated here.

'Either you are modest, or you are a fool, Johannes. But, if you have business, I shall not force you to stand on ceremony in my house. Your time is doubtless limited,' she said in turn to her son-in-law and me.

'I am grateful for your hospitality,' I added.

'Yes, well,' Monsieur Vermeer said, perhaps a little embarrassed by this unusually candid exchange. 'Let us go through to the inner kitchen.'

As I had sensed, the house was large, with many rooms whose exact purpose I might not at first guess. Only at the end of our view down the corridor was I aware of natural light, and it was from there that a great sound of children shouting came. However, on the way, as I passed through the front hall, my eyes were held by the sight of a most interesting canvas that looked somehow familiar. I believed I had seen it recently, yet not in this form. I judged it to be in the Utrecht style, as were some other works I saw on the walls. In fact, I saw so many pictures within just this reception area that my mind wandered back to that strange visit and viewing of Monsieur Vermeer's own works at Monsieur van Ruijven's. Again, in some instances, I had to ask myself where the painted images ended and where the actual architecture of life in these Dutch houses began.

I think Monsieur Vermeer noticed the extent to which I was distracted ... He looked at me with amusement, and placed his hand on my arm to steer me upstairs.

'I have come to a decision, one that has weighed heavily on me since your unexpected but welcome arrival. What I ask of you is not without risk. It is that you should indeed attend the conclave and hear of the discovery that has been made. There is no possibility that we can disguise your nationality, but since the discoverer is anyway . . .'

Here, he stopped himself, evidently not prepared to betray his secret in its entirety.

'Suffice to say that there are only a handful of people who know of this matter.'

I thought that a door was opening somewhere in my mind, that I in fact might already have some knowledge of what he was alluding to here, but I could not gain unimpeded access.

'We have a heavy task ahead of us at this meeting and I hold responsibility beyond that which with I will ever be comfortable.'

I wanted to add my thoughts to this tantalising speech, but he went on.

'But in any case, I feel, from what I can see from your genuine interest in the field of science and art, and especially our art, that it would be unfair to rob you of this opportunity to witness such an event.'

Perhaps, I thought, and I did not dare to put this into words, he wanted a witness unconnected with this community that had given rise to such a gathering.

'When is this meeting?' I said, with perhaps too great alacrity.

'It is tonight.'

'That is soon indeed.'

He sat back in his chair, a weight lifted from him.

I took in this second, sparser painting room of his. The tiles were familiar to me, as were the mullioned windows. But more than this, I could not but stand back and be amazed at the handsome virginal, which, like the tiles and windows, I saw to be the one depicted in his current painting in his mother's inn.

'The painting means much to you?' I inquired, perhaps a little boldly.

I remembered the shackled image of Pero, his hands behind his back.

'I knew Catharina for many years before we were finally able to marry,' he said, as if he had misheard me, like an old man who launches unbidden into tales of his childhood.

'Her mother was the chief obstacle, as you can imagine. Or did you not know that I was born a Protestant?'

'I was told.'

'Indeed. If there is any one picture I can leave Catharina or my children, as a testament, it will be this one.'

'But surely you are not ill, to be preoccupied with such things?'

'Oh, no. Thank you for your concern. But I am perhaps a little afraid.'

I had the feeling that he would resist my inquiries as to the real nature of this particular work. What was one to make, after all, of the image of the bonded man sucking milk at the breast of his daughter, whilst in the main picture another, much younger man deferred to the young lady, who was turned away from him, her concentration ambiguous, her reflected image indeed, uncertain. And that small blurred triangular image in the corner of the mirror?

'I have the impression, and I hope that I am not trespassing here on a private matter, but I feel, such is my captivation by your present work, I feel that there is an unhappy mood in your household.'

He looked at me in a most astonished fashion, but I pressed on. 'Yet how can that be, when there should be rejoicing?'

'It is the reflection that troubles her so much. I intended it to be Catharina's, but I cannot get Maritje's from my head. And so the evidence is there. I am condemned by my own art.'

Thus far only was I prepared to intrude. Whatever Maritje meant to him was not my concern here. And it appeared to me that Catharina was indisputably a woman and a mother to be cherished and upheld as the person of most profound meaning in his life.

'When it is dark we will gather inside the Prinsenhof,' he said. 'Shall we agree to meet there?'

'Indeed, nothing would prevent me.'

He took me down to the entrance, and we bade a brief goodbye, Monsieur Vermeer understandably anxious to save time and prepare for whatever it was to which I would be witness that evening.

It was my first visit to the Prinsenhof, situated behind the Oude Kerk to the west of the town, and I almost regretted that the conclave was to take place at such an hour. I would have liked to explore this concatenation of buildings, rooms, and passages and see its many rooms and decorations at my leisure. Yet what secrets would this place yield to me on this special night? I had arrived early, and had been admitted into the main hall. I supposed from the demeanour of the few officials and guards about that word had been given them to let me wander as I wished. Presently, however, I noticed a steady stream of gentlemen arrive and proceed down a corridor of the building. These figures did not seem to need guidance of any kind, nor were they checked in any way except by the most cursory of glances. Did I know some of these faces passing by me, like familiar portraits? Certainly, as this procession continued at short intervals, I became convinced I had seen some of these personages before, and it was soon clear to me, like someone at a dinner who has not noticed that one may proceed with eating, that the conclave of painters and scientists was about to begin.

Then, to my relief, Monsieur Vermeer arrived, and took me down that same corridor. At the end of the corridor we went through a door which led directly into a narrow, bare passage which turned right, then left, and right once more, so that I think I had already lost my sense of place. I found it hard to imagine that so many notable personages had preceded us down this rather undignified route.

Yet when we came out, it was to witness a sight, the substance of which I have withheld from you too long, my dear son, and the like of which I knew then I was never again to witness. Before me was a long hall, divided by a table, on either side of which were ranged two groups of gentlemen I immediately took to be painters, most of whom were dressed as well as might be any wealthy Dutch trader from Amsterdam. The whole scene reminded me of one of master Rembrandt van Rijn's portraits of eminent burghers.

Then I saw Borry, looking haggard and even more haunted than when I had last seen him; I saw Huygens, who stood surveying the assembled company with an air of regal pride and circumspection; I saw Van Ruijven also, who had about him an air of weary impatience. In particular I noticed Gerard Dou, from Leiden, squinting through his eyeglasses in the low light of the room. Then there were those fleeting faces I had noticed on the way to this meeting, those half-familiar features which I felt I had seen in other sizes and dimensions, and indeed in other apparel. I turned to Monsieur Vermeer, like one who, after searching many years for a treasure, has been humbled and chastened by a sight too rich for his eyes.

'Many of the assembled company I believe I have seen, yet I cannot say with any certainty . . .'

'You will learn soon enough, but it might be useful to make you aware, it is true,' he said. 'There, for example, are two friends of mine, Samuel van Hoogstraten—he has rather large, kindly eyes (I noted too his long, rather feminine eyelashes)—and beside him, Nicolaes Maes. I shall be particularly keen to hear Hoogstraten's views.'

'They were pupils of Van Rijn, I believe?'

'Yes, like Fabritius, they all knew each other. And then, that handsome man looking somewhat like a cavalier, with the moustache, you see there Ger . . .'

'Gerard Terborch!'

'And Leeuwenhoek, of course,' at which the avuncular-looking microscopist nodded, as if he had detected his name across all the busy muttering and jocular discourse.

'And De Witte, and . . .'

Here his attention fell on a figure just entering who might have been described as well dressed had his clothes not looked slightly dishevelled, his hair a little unkempt.

'Oh, well, I find it hard to believe. It is Pieter de Hooch. Finally returned to Delft! I had heard he has been most successful since his move.'

I thought I detected for the first time in Monsieur Vermeer's voice a note of sarcasm.

'Yes, I remember. Yet he does not look well, do you not think, Mijn Heer Vermeer?'

'He looks different, it is true.'

'And these painters, they do not live in Delft?' I said by way of asking for an explanation for these illustrious presences.

'No, you are right. Some have come from far away, and many have suspended their work on important commissions. Take Hoogstraten, for example, he is currently working in England.'

The arrival of more distinguished gentlemen, all of them Dutch, apart from Monsieur Borry and myself, I noted, continued for quite some time so that soon the atmosphere in the hall became sultry. When I suggested opening a window, I was warned of the utter secrecy of this meeting and that such an action posed a risk of eavesdropping and even spying. This last was said by Monsieur Huygens, whom I thought much less disposed to me than on previous occasions, though I sensed that he had more weighing on him than was to be expected from a simple meeting of painters. It was soon after this that everyone assembled was indeed called upon to direct his attention to the matter at hand.

'Gentlemen,' Huygens began, 'I thank you all for your coming here tonight, for many of you at some expense and not insignificant inconvenience. I need hardly say, I hope, that there could not have been any other time or indeed place to discuss the weighty matter at hand. Whatever the outcome, I am certain that you will not go away this morning to your separate and worthy pursuits disappointed. I know that many of you, like myself, have a penchant for spectacle . . .'

He halted while a brief flurry of amusement passed around the hall, along with a respectful acknowledgement in the direction of the portly Hoogstraten.

'And that penchant will be gratified, but there is a

more serious matter for consideration, one that will require a vow of secrecy from you all. And lest it be transgressed . . . well, you know *that* condition.'

He conveyed this last, veiled statement with great reluctance and not a little personal anguish, as he surveyed the faces ranged to his left and right. I knew then that I should not be afraid. This was a man of position and trust who would take no pleasure in abusing such a status. And it seemed also to me that this could not have been the first occasion on which all these persons had come together to hear such a warning, as no shock was registered on any face that I could see.

'I shall take it that, unless any of you now wishes to express dissent in this matter, you are all from this moment bound by this vow, a vow of silence.'

To be sure, there could be heard the slightest of nervous mumblings at these words, but the general consensus was one of acquiescence, if not impatience, to know more.

'The discussion will be of an optical engine such as none of us could have till now imagined, and to dismiss any scepticism there will be a demonstration in your presence later tonight. But first I must call upon one of you to assist us in this matter.'

There was a moment of expectation, as if one of us would be called upon to engage in something perilous, from which there was a general, palpable shying away. But Huygens knew whom he wanted. He turned to me.

'Monsieur de Monconys. You occupy a position in tonight's affairs the importance of which I do not think you can have known.'

'I, Sir? I am afraid I do not understand. I was only invited here this very day.'

'Yes, indeed. However, I must now call on you to

submit the document you received from Monsieur Borry. He has been able to show us much, but without the details he recorded we cannot go through with this so necessary demonstration.'

Monsieur Borry looked at me glumly, as if to say there was nothing we could do about this situation.

'The guards will escort you back to your lodgings . . .'

Then it was the turn of Monsieur Vermeer.

'Mijn Heer Huygens. There will be no need for that. I shall accompany Monsieur de Monconys myself. He is after all my guest.'

'Very well, we shall set up the necessary equipment, as we await your return.'

We returned to my room in Monsieur Vermeer's house. Before we entered, as we passed the Nieuwe Kerk, I thought he stopped and looked towards his house as if contemplating some terrible, regretful event. I wondered if he was considering asking me to flee for fear of endangering myself further, but he continued on. I retrieved the document from my wallet there, a document to which I had admittedly given scant attention till now, and we hastened back to the building.

We arrived back to find the distinguished assembly in an uproar, of which Borry seemed to be at the centre.

'There is no trickery here, as much as some of you like to claim is your own goal,' he said, looking at Hoogstraten. 'For, you yourself have often said, the aim of art is to deceive the eye.'

Hoogstraten smiled indulgently.

A sheet of paper was being passed around the room, and going through the hands of the disbelieving painters and scientists. When it finally reached myself and Monsieur Vermeer, I recognised the peculiarly spectral image

Borry had shown me in The Hague of a figure standing in the *voorhuis* of a house, and with it, I was reminded of the technique for which I had seen no precedent. It could not be called a drawing; another material had been employed. Nor could it be described as a picture in oils, because the surface texture had a quality I had never seen before. To wit, there was no colour; there was a strange depth that exceeded the achievements of any illusion I had hitherto witnessed even in Holland; and there was not the customary sheen that is discerned in almost every oil picture. There *was* no word for it, short of magic, a word I was highly reluctant to use. I did not know what I should conclude from Monsieur Vermeer's thoughtful silence.

'Well, it is most strange, but this looks to me like some trickery of Hoogstraten's,' old Dou said, peering at the image with quite some difficulty, I thought, before he turned towards the painter he had just named, 'though I say this with the greatest admiration.'

'I am honoured, sir, but this is no work of mine. Besides, my eyes . . .'

Borry drew himself up. 'I knew that you might not be convinced by this example alone; it is unperfected, and not so recent,' he countered. 'Therefore I have in mind to prove to you all that I am no charlatan. However, I shall not be able to demonstrate to you the exact sequence of the process, no more than I could show you the glazing of porcelain from within the oven, simply because that part, we might call it the second stage, has to be performed in complete darkness. In any case, we may not proceed until dawn.'

'Till dawn indeed,' I heard Dou say, as if his age and position were being personally affronted.

'One might ask what Mijn Heer Vermeer thinks of all this,' Leeuwenhoek challenged.

'Or indeed yourself,' Huygens added. I, as everyone, was well aware of his current progress with lenses. But Leeuwenhoek did not have the opportunity to comment on Huygens' teasing words.

'I do not presume to know more than anyone here present,' Monsieur Vermeer responded calmly. 'But I think we ignore a discovery such as this at our peril.'

'In any case, everything is in place,' Huygens said, calling everyone to order.

An hour or more was passed in discussion that ranged from Alhazen, Witelo, Bacon, Leonardo, Viator, Dürer, Kepler, Marolois, Hondius, to De Vries. Hoogstraten even had time to show us an example of his own work. He did this by asking me to walk over to the room in the far corner where a door had been opened, perhaps to let in some air, allowing a view of a corridor, off which various chambers led, much as in a wealthy patrician household, and where a springer spaniel boldly looked over the threshold at us, whilst, further down, I noticed two figures in discussion. It was only when I was perhaps three feet from my destination that I realised and stopped. What I had taken to be another room and a view down a corridor was exactly that, just a view, but one painted on canvas and placed against the wall. Very soon everyone in the hall gave a hearty chuckle of knowing amusement. I knew then that Hoogstraten had used the opportunity of my short absence to uncover the painted panel standing against the wall. I was happy that a light-hearted nonsense could be tolerated in such circumstances as these; I suspected it had been performed as much to lighten the atmosphere as to demonstrate the many talents of this man, who, I heard it whispered, was currently writing his own treatise on perspective.

When true light finally did arrive, I saw a familiar

scene revealed along the length of the hall. Strong rods of diagonal light entered through the crested leaded window closest to the back wall. Against this wall now stood Maritje, the young model I had seen in Monsieur Vermeer's house some days before.

Everyone was invited to approach the woman and study her face, her pearl earrings, her black and yellow top, until they were content. They had to divide their curiosity between the woman's natural beauty and the box, which I took to be a camera obscura, which Borry had mounted on a stand in front of her. She was asked to pose for many minutes without moving before she was thanked and dismissed. Borry then seemed to take something from his box, and disappeared into a room at the other end of the hall, which I noted was unlit, and from which he did not emerge for another hour. By the time he did, the previous atmosphere of clandestine excitement had mostly faded, and some people were even beginning to droop in their chairs—if they were not already asleep.

However, when he did reappear, Borry's face was beaming so much that it did not take very long for his excitement to be conveyed around the room. He was holding up what looked to be a small portrait of the woman we had seen standing by the window.

'Gentlemen, if you will,' he said, walking over to the window. Before he could say any more, Huygens took the object from him and looked on it as if he thought he would see his own future there.

'You must hold it in the light,' was the only instruction he was allowed to utter. Huygens held the image, which I saw was mounted under a glass plate, up against the light of the window, and it was a strange effect indeed. It showed a face, perhaps even a woman's face, but not as one is accustomed to see it. It seemed to me that every area that should be light was dark and every area intended to be dark was light.

'Monsieur Borry, what is this curiosity? I hope this is not the final product of your work?'

'Mijn Heer Huygens, if I may be permitted.'

Here Borry took the panel from Huygens' hand and held it not against the light, but at an angle, in such a way that the light was reflected off it. Silence descended over everyone then as they hung on Huygens' reaction, though some of those nearest to him, including myself, were actually witness to what he could see.

'Borry, if this be no trick and you no charlatan, then all painting is dead.'

'And the effect, Mijn Heer,' Borry said, hardly responding to the ominous pronouncement of that distinguished man of letters and science, 'will be all the greater if I place this velvet card to the back of the glass.'

I saw what Huygens saw, and I can only describe what I felt as fear, as if I were regarding a spirit, the miniaturised revenant of the woman who had been standing by the window just an hour before. Yet this fear remained for no more than a few passing moments because its place was soon taken by that of wonder. There was here both a superb, fine flatness to the surface of the image, a detail in certain areas that was greater than nature herself and a softness in places, especially in the earrings and in the whites of the girl's eyes that I had never known before that day. And the further from the image I drew back, the sharper did the whole become.

After the image had been seen by everyone present, each to his entire satisfaction, Huygens said simply to Borry, 'We have much to discuss, but I shall ask you to wait for our decision.'

Whereupon, Borry was escorted out by two guards,

and the remaining members looked around at each other as if in embarrassed collusion.

'We have to consider how to proceed, gentlemen. That is our first task here.'

Huygens' words brought the assembly abruptly to order.

'We see this as our duty to report this to the proper authorities,' someone said.

'But we are an unofficial authority ourselves. We cannot run the risk of exposing ourselves,' Leeuwenhoek retorted. 'I think rather it is an aesthetic matter that we have to discuss here.'

'That granted, sir, it would be perilous to overlook the military implications, especially when the source of this discovery is a Frenchman, with all due respect to Monsieur de Monconys.'

Huygens acknowledged me once more, though I rather wished he had not; I would have preferred to have disappeared into one of Monsieur Vermeer's dark rooms than have attention once again directed my way. I was only here, after all, to witness, as Leeuwenhoek the scientist ironically pointed out, the aesthetic significance of this invention.

'It must be put to the vote,' another voice offered.

'The question is, will this method truly help the painter or will it replace him completely?' Huygens proffered.

'What about the guilds?'

'Perspective is dead.'

'The painter has colour.'

'The two can exist together; they will complement and enhance each other.'

'They will halt the development of oil pictures for ever.'

'People are not ready for this kind of magic; they will resist it.'

'The guilds will not allow it.'

The comments issued from sundry members of this illustrious gathering, all a variation on the same theme. I think that by the end of this mêlée, Monsieur Vermeer was the only one who had failed to make his position clear.

'We shall, as suggested earlier, put this to the vote,' Huygens interrupted softly. It was enough to bring everyone to order. 'I shall ask you gentlemen to make your opinions formally known. Simply put, you gentlemen must decide if what we have seen today should be made public or should, as far as it is in our power, never be reproduced again. Therefore, I call upon all of you to make your position known, for or against.' Here, he took in his breath here.

'Those who agree that it should be made public raise your hand.'

There was a count.

'Twenty.'

'Those who agree that it should remain unknown.'

'Twenty.'

To everyone's astonishment, Monsieur Huygens counted the hands again.

'Has anyone not voted?'

People looked around until eventually a common line of sight was agreed on. And I became aware (I and Monsieur Borry, along with Monsieur Huygens, were naturally excluded from the vote) that the object of everyone's regard was the person standing next to me, Monsieur Vermeer.

'Sir, you have not voted?'

'No.'

'Do you wish to remain neutral in this matter?'
'I . . .'
'Because no neutral position is possible. We must decide today, this morning.'

Monsieur Vermeer offered no reply.

Huygens gave out a sigh of slight irritation.

'Monsieur Vermeer, are you for or against the thing?'

'I believe that the invention may be of inestimable use to painters.'

'But?'

'We should not be asked to decide in this matter.'

'But, Sir. You have no choice.'

'Then I shall vote against the making public of it.'

'Thank you, Mijn Heer.'

We were sworn to secrecy, and I believe that Monsieur Vermeer and many of the painters present were regretful beyond measure in having to assume the positions that they had finally taken. It was as if they had committed a crime against art, but it was one they had committed in great part to protect their own countrymen and livelihoods.

I left the very stuffy atmosphere of the secret room with Monsieur Vermeer through a private doorway, feeling as if he were my only protection. I knew that I had to leave and never come back to this country again, as, were I to do so, I might easily find myself faced with false charges of espionage. I felt as if I was damned. Though I knew that in my normal itinerary I would have little opportunity to visit here on very many subsequent occasions, still it was as if I had been deprived of the use of a limb, or an eye even.

We crossed the Oude Delft canal, passed by the

Oude Kerk, walked along the Hippolytusbuurt, where the home of the lens maker, Monsieur Leeuwenhoek, was to be found, and then we passed behind the Town Hall. It was still very early, but there were already several market sellers and traders on their way to the Great Market.

It was as we walked through a walled pathway of red brick and came to a corner that I heard voices that seemed to be grumbling and muttering, and were then suspended for a few moments as if coming upon some revelation. We walked on, to find a small patch of green on which lay various white sheets and I saw the crowd. They were gathered around a figure lying prostrate on one of these sheets. This uncommon sight would have been enough to arrest my attention alone, even though I had not thought the clothes of the poor person familiar, as I think too did Monsieur Vermeer. It was a woman, to be sure, lying face down on one of the sheets, and a man was pulling her up by the shoulder and arm. It was a sight I hope never to witness again. The face could only be described as ravaged, by what chemical abomination I could only guess at. It was as if the woman's very skin had been erased, making her features void. I felt Monsieur Vermeer hold on to my arm, the thought arriving with him at the same time as with me.

'It is Maritje,' he whispered. Before I could question such knowledge, he urged, 'We must go.'

'But we must take her home!' I found myself protesting.

'My dear Monconys, do you not realize the danger we face?' he whispered, harshly. His expression was a mixture of horror, astonishment, fear ... but above all of determination. I think no one would have noticed our abrupt departure, so transfixed were they by the horrific sight.

We went straight to his painting room. Only the maid had stirred as yet.

'It was the conclave,' he said. 'And this is something terrible. I am to blame for her death. And who knows what might be the fate of poor Borry if this is what happens to Maritje?'

'You may well be right about Borry but you could not know the intentions of such people.'

'If I had not objected, she would be still be alive.'

'You do not know that.'

'Now Catharina can have her way.'

'You mean the painting?'

So as to quieten my own inner turmoil after the horrific sight I had just seen, I found myself attending to every detail of the painting that Monsieur Vermeer was working away at so feverishly now. Despite his uncommon concentration on the task, I noticed that his hand trembled from time to time, so that eventually he rose and brought back with him a maulstick for resting one hand on. To be sure, he was not unaffected by the so recent and terrible sight of Maritje, or I should rather say negation of sight, and I saw the tiniest beads of sweat, like moons in parallel orbit, moving down that absorbed and furrowed brow. And now I saw that although the painting as a whole had progressed very slowly, there was one area, that of the reflection in the mirror, where the work had advanced greatly. The reflection of the woman I had known as Maritje was achingly clear, as clear as the thin bevelled edge at the bottom of the mirror itself that formed a kind of frame within a frame. In that square could also be seen the leg of the painter's own easel, a device I had thought rather superfluous, though not uncommon in this type of work, except that now, after what I had seen of Borry's invention and Monsieur Vermeer's camera obscura,

I could only see its inclusion as inseparable from the whole.

Now he took up his brush, dipped it into some colours on his palette, and daubed the face until it was but a warm blur. It was nothing now.

'Catharina has her wish.'

I had not noticed until now the intensity of the murmurs coming from the street outside, doubtless occasioned by the discovery of the dead woman. I wondered how long it would take until the peace of this sanctuary would be broken.

'You should go now. Do not worry about me.'

'You will finish the picture?' I said, as if without his acquiescence I could not leave, though I fully expected the town militia, of which Monsieur Vermeer was himself a member, to come hammering at the door.

'I shall finish it. It is Catharina's treasure.'

At his door, I thought of offering my condolences, but it seemed inappropriate; it would be only a way of adding to his woes and the violence with which our short-lived friendship must now be ended. So I said finally, 'I thank you, most solemnly, and I wish you well.'

I walked straight into the anonymity of the Great Market Square and it seemed to me that the earlier commotion had already died down and that everyone was going about their business. However, on the way, standing on the corner of a street, I saw, for the last time, Pieter Claesz. van Ruijven. I thought at first that he met my gaze directly, but he did not acknowledge me, so that I am forced now to wonder whether he saw me at all.

What happened to me from then on, once I had reached The Hague and the protection of the Duke, is of little consequence. It is in any case well documented in my journals.

What I have imparted to you here is to be made of and employed by you as you see fit.
Your loving father,
                    Balthasar de Monconys

Part three:

*Reconstruction*

'Don't be too busy for dead paint'

*Spoken to the art forger Derwatt, in Wim Wenders'* The American Friend *(Der Amerikanische Freund), based on the Patricia Highsmith novel,* Ripley's Game

Yes, I did find the document and it's now with a well-known organisation for evaluation. I've had it translated for your convenience. You will have to judge its authenticity for yourself. Suffice to say that it was a stroke of luck, almost too good to be true. Well, it wasn't quite perfect, because the formula that Borry talks about, whatever that is exactly, is not included in Monconys' document. There, I've said it, I've lain it out baldly and told you what I'm about, as easily as that. The mystery is over, you're thinking.

Well, not really. Though right at the outset, and before continuing I should state for the record that I am not a forger, a faker or any other alliterative term you might be tempted to coin. I copy, I sometimes clean, and my talents are wide-ranging. I got into this whole thing because I agreed to make a copy of a Vermeer.

Actually, I really do have a sneaking affection for M. de Monconys. He was not only so close to a painter he had developed an instinctive liking for—let's face it, he could have written the first monograph on Vermeer—and to the greatest discovery of his time, and yet this very proximity and the exclusivity of what he was privileged to witness denied him any chance of exploiting what he had found out.

They asked me to copy *The Music Lesson*. I did not know what it would involve. It's late afternoon. Outside the house, a lozenge of orange light is stretched out across the back wall of my studio and some teenagers from the local housing estate are hanging suspiciously around my car. I stupidly left a painting in there, covered up, of course, but I'm damned if I'm going to go out there and make a fool of myself. I was *asked* to copy it. I've been asked to copy many paintings but I have never come close to losing my sanity or my wife on any of these occasions. But who would not take the opportunity to work on, I should say work with, their favourite painter? When *I* do so, I immerse myself in his or her world—completely. You might find it easy to recognise the particular work I am talking of, but I am not so sure. I don't think I'm that worried any more, I know they could come for me any time now, just as they could have and probably did go after Monconys two years after his departure from Delft when he suddenly died.

Dear Reader, before your prejudices allow themselves to take a hold of you, I am not Van Meegeren. My initials do not betray an illusion such as did the poor famous forger's. IVM. Jan Ver Meer. Jan Van Meegeren. Hah! In any case, I cannot tell you my name; that would really put the cat among the pigeons.

Actually, I made *two* copies simultaneously so that I would have something to show for my efforts at the end of the day, apart from the money. I am looking at it now. I would love to see their faces if they suddenly turned up and saw me gazing at a replica of their own replica. It's only a matter of time before they realize that the 'original' is not their stolen painting after all and that it's really in the Queen's possession and will at some stage doubtless resurface in the Royal Collection or in one of the travelling road shows that her Majesty sometimes allows herself. I should have given that more thought. I hadn't reckoned with those *agents* cocking the whole thing up. Don't ask me how; it's enough to know that it went wrong, surely? Yes, they offered me a new identity and relocation and all that, but that would mean . . . Now this is my only solace, along with what I remember of Sophie, my photographs and paintings of her.

Somehow the moment came for me to be escorted for the first of many sessions in front of the original in the cool back room of that illustrious building. My life finally made sense for the first time. I was so close to him, I was privileged, as privileged as the Frenchman when he sat in Vermeer's studio and saw the very pigments the painter had used, breathing in the very life of the artist's immediate surroundings. But when I was with *him*, I was away from Sophie. Of course I was back with her in the evenings, when I would repeat my work for my own copy. So I was never really with them both. I cannot say when I first developed my theories. I am not really a writer; but then, neither am I an academic. I just like to collect knowledge, as much as things. And I'm an inveterate cataloguer, a 'completist' if you will.

Vermeer took me around the world and led me to Sophie. He also lost her for me. Thanks very much, Johannes. My task is as much curatorial nowadays as creative. As I said, I am not a writer and I do not know how to tell you our story, except in terms of his work. That is possible, if on the face of it unlikely.

However, before we go on, there are some things I should mention for you to mull over as you read. Who am I writing this for?

1. An art journal.
2. A literary magazine
3. Myself. I could be mad.

4. The narrator(s), with whom I am in collusion to totally confuse you.
5. An art book. It is a personal meditation on all things Vermeer, intended as the introduction to a monograph on the painter by a very good and trusted friend of mine.
6. A museum catalogue.
7. A letter to an art-loving friend, or to Sophie.
8. A manual on how to copy a Vermeer painting successfully, not how to fake one.
9. A little of all of these.
10. None of these.

# *The Music Lesson—A Copyist's Manual*

*The plain-weave linen support has a thread count of 15 x 14 per cm². The original tacking edges have been removed. Cusping occurs on all sides, more pronounced along top and bottom edges. The canvas has been lined. The light brownish grey ground contains lead white, chalk, and a little umber, with aggregates of lead white particles. The paint is thinly and smoothly applied although some texture is present, as on the nearest edge of the bass viol, which stands out due to curling impasto. The bottom half of the painting has a strong blue cast. The dark tiles in the foreground are blue while those further back in the composition are dark grey and contain no blue pigment. The shadow of the carpet on the table in the right foreground is dominated by a bright blue, which may be discoloured. A pinhole with which Vermeer marked the vanishing point of the composition is visible in the paint layer.*[1]

Is it not poetry? Read it enough times with that painting in mind, and it is. I have a weakness and envy for such technical, supposedly cold language.

*The Art of Painting,* measuring 120 x 100 cm, has one particular aspect in common with *The Music Lesson.* It depicts, amongst other things, an artist's easel, almost in full, except where it disappears behind the artist's body. The same is true of the canvas itself, which also hides behind the artist and becomes indistinguishable from the back wall that it depicts, as clever as, and a good deal subtler than, anything Magritte ever pulled off.

The other common, albeit exterior, aspect is that fate conspired to allow me to cement the acquaintance I had struck up with Sophie in front of the one picture in Vienna with the welcome coincidence of meeting her again in front of the other in London. It was as if the intervening period, when I had travelled around Europe and America on my self-imposed tour, was the ground[2] for our own canvas, stretched across the intervening countries.

Doubtless our paths could have converged earlier, like the lines in one of De Vries' charming perspective drawings, but perhaps if they had, the timing would not have been as propitious as it turned out to be, snapping a connection that had barely been established.

### The Stretcher

I prefer to make my own. You need a support, of course, which you assemble from five separate sections, the main rectangle established by slotting together four mitre grooved joints to allow small wedges to be tapped into them to give the canvas the springiness that will play its inevitable part in what is at heart a biological process.

You buy the weave of your desire, but a fine weave is best, and tack that to the support frame (no easy matter, that), making sure that the weave is parallel to the lowest bar even at the corners. I prefer good canvas pliers to get as firm a grip as possible. You add the size[3], then leave it a few days to dry. I am not making any attempt to replicate an aged canvas or support, as I did at the Gallery. For *them*. I am not a faker. (Don't forget, though, that even in Vermeer's time there were professional copyists.)


**Vienna, The Model**

It might be romantic for Strauss lovers or decadent for Schiele and Klimt aficionados, but for me it is a city whose purpose is to contain a museum which houses a masterpiece by Vermeer. At first I was startled by its size—its format is less square than many of his other works—more than by its darkness. I was making sketches, more adaptations than faithful representations, seeing what I could do with certain motifs.

I was still a bit dreamily lost in my own reminiscences of a few years earlier when I had been on another trek across Europe with a university friend. That had been pleasant in parts, except when Mark had insisted on dragging me to a concentration camp. A public schoolboy, he still had not got past the stage of wanting to outrage me, whom he thought still sheltered and a little introverted. Maybe I was, but I was romantic too. That time, too, I had ended up letting Mark convince me to go to a prostitute with him, an unwise decision, for me at least. Years later, he would try to justify it with arguments along the lines that a good artist, and certainly a specialist in a prostitute-saturated area such as Dutch art, has to see the world and experience life.

'It was part of life then,' Mark argued, 'it was and is part of the iconography . . .' He had a point.

But for now I was absorbed in the painting before me. One strange thing about the modern era of art appreciation is that we are so used to seeing familiar paintings reproduced in books in all combinations of light exposure that we are often shocked to see the state the actual work is in, how it is lit, even how it is hung. These concerns sometimes take over from the

*The Dance of Geometry*

more prevalent, perhaps more important aspects of interpretation. I am naturally interested in both, yet perhaps more than that, I am held captive by the original state of something, its original proportions, the realness or not of whatever is depicted. In Vermeer, this is dangerous territory, since he mixes in the probably real, like the map in the Vienna painting which still exists in Paris, with objects or places that have been taken from other locations, often objects that were probably never in his studio. Even De Hooch did this.

That morning in the museum, it was the map that I was concentrating on. On the replication of a triptych of vertical folds, on the subtle shadows that were falling over the northern part of Holland (it is to be remembered that only ten years later Holland would be at war again, with France, and that Vermeer would suffer a series of financial disasters), and the series of tiny cartouches of the towns and cities that made up the Seven States of Holland and in this painting surround the main map like film frame sprockets.

Slowly, stealthily, your attention shifts from the map to the figure of the woman with the book and the trumpet. The leaves of her laurel crown are the only things that the painter has so far succeeded in finishing and the colour code of her dress is almost subliminally echoed in reverse on the theatrical curtain that opens up onto this studio scene. The blue leaves, of course, were originally green. They are blue now, as a result of oxidization.

I was sketching the figure of the model. You cannot but admire how she is framed (in Vermeer almost everything is framed a second time, within the conventional physical frame) by the corner of the map. Vermeer's signature is visible to the immediate right of her collar but it is written as if it is a signature on the map: a horizontal dark blue border running from the bottom of the map at the seated artist's eye level to the puffed-out collar of her robe, just before which we can see his own signature,

IVMeer. Meanwhile, the model's head is almost perfectly bisected by the vertical line of the inside border; this invisible intersection pins her to that corner. I don't know which concerned me more— the negative space surrounding her, the strict conformity of rectangular lines that made everything almost three-dimensional, or the snakelike pattern of folds and shadows in her dress.

Only then did I become aware of a real, double shadow, hovering over the manufactured, interpreted ones on my pad. I did not look up. I really did not want any distractions. Secretly, I feared the moment some uncharitable warden would take it into his or her head to prevent me from continuing. Whoever it was, was staring unapologetically at my sketch, concentrating on some area I could not detect.

'The ascending blue leaves,' she said, as if reciting a line of poetry.

At this, I had to look up.

Her voice, which, apart from her shadow, had been my first acquaintance with her, was plummy and rounded. It did not fit the face; I almost caught myself looking around to check if it hadn't come from somewhere else.

'I'm sorry?' I said. The phrase rang a bell, but, like the delay that preceded fitting her voice to the face, I did not at first make the obvious connection with the painting. Perhaps I was in shock. Women this beautiful just don't come up to you in galleries, especially when you are doing something as pretentious as copying a master.

'Why are they blue? Do you know?'

'It's because the original green paint has oxidized.'

'Oxiwhat?'

'The yellow part of the green has gradually reacted with the air, oxygen, you . . .'

'Ach, Sauerstoff. Now I see,' she continues, 'but blue is better.'

'It wasn't intended.'

'But it has always been blue . . .'
Was she trying to be obtuse or was she just thick?
'But that's just the point, it hasn't always been blue.'
And then it happened, like a camera focusing slowly on its subject. Her face had just enough of that friendly smirk, her lips the fullness, her jaw that European angularity, to betray her own fascination in the painting.
'Do you work in the museum?' she said, motioning at the sketch.
'I'm doing research.' I cringed. It sounded so fake. It *was* research, but it was hardly as if I really knew what I was doing yet.
'Oh, for what?'
'For some paintings I'm doing, using Vermeer.'
As I was saying this, the thought was stealing up on me, the obviousness of which I was still denying to myself. This was only the beginning of my project. Was I to start hankering after the first woman I had noticed? But then, the resemblance . . . She was studying German language and literature, *Germanistik*, but she was already considering modelling work. She had had plenty of offers. It was her fifth year, and she was intensely interested in her PhD subject, the poetry of Georg Trakl. I had never heard of him.

**The Ground**

Take the sized canvas. Here I am skipping a few very important stages—you have already applied the gesso and smoothed the canvas down, after which you have applied the oil primer, and likewise sanded down. Apply the first layer, the imprimatura— lead white, chalk, and a little umber, as per the original, as far as we can guess. You squeeze the colours out of the tubes onto the canvas, take a rag dipped in turps, and use this to spread the paint across and into the whole canvas. This stage is really the clue as to how the whole thing will turn out, since it will give you the overall tone to the picture. I like to think of it as the first significant conversation you have with the person who later turns out to be your partner. You can read into it the future of your relationship (which you could not have done at the time, of course), had you even thought to stop for a second. But we're more in control here, surely.

'Would you model for *me*?'
A burst of surprised laughter, followed by an unconscious touching of the hollow under your chin.
'Is it such a shock?'
Soon I realised that this was one of your characteristic responses.
'It won't involve nudity,' I hastened to add. Another burst of laughter, another testing of that negative space, the hand hanging there like a rock climber under a horizontal ledge.
'Do you have a studio in Vienna?'
'No, but . . . I'm only doing sketches at this stage. I can do them almost anywhere.'
We were sitting in a café in the Old Town, trams rattling by a few feet from the window; you were on your way to the library.
'OK. You can come to my flat. It's near the Prater.'
'When?' I asked her, hardly daring to breathe.
'Tomorrow?' said Sophie, with adorable simplicity. 'I'll draw you a map."

I still have it. She drew on a napkin with a ball pen. Though it's barely legible now, it's as valuable to me as any painting I've done of her. I'm looking into ways of preserving it better, using chemicals, putting it eventually under glass. I've photographed it too, and made a print of it.

## The Dance of Geometry

*It's strange but looking at her then, you imagine the worst happening to beauty.*

### Delft, Research

On a bus now, near empty, with only a couple of teenagers at the back. The bus is meandering through flat fields framed by drainage ditches and intermittent canals.

On the way to a small village, Schipluiden (Schipluy, as it was then), where Jan was married to Catharina. The church, of course, is no longer there. Why should I in fact expect anything to be the same, except maybe the sky? What was the weather like that day? Somehow the clarity and flatness of the landscape seems as if it has been laid out for me to ease my search. Do you think she is here?

That day in April, they would have walked for about an hour from Delft in a quiet, modest procession, the Bolnes' side of the family wedding party wary about displaying their religion too ostentatiously. Jan's heart might have sunk at the sight of Gerard Terborch turning up just like that. Was he mocking him? A sunny but still bitterly cold day, with Jan feeling he had overcome the greatest battle. True, there was still Maria Thins to win over, but he was confident: he loved Catharina.

I get off the bus, which stops beside a narrow canal, opposite a row of small shops. Precious little to indicate a relation with the famous painter except, on the door of a local baker's, a reproduction of the milkmaid with that huge jug which never seems to get any heavier.

I locate the only old church, its history uncertain, but do not get inside. It's not the one, anyway. What was it Sophie said about the painting in the Mauritshuis at The Hague, *Girl with a Pearl Earring* (44.5 x 39 cm, almost square), 'a lower lip shining like a tiny waterfall'? After that she could not say anything wrong.


## *Underpainting*

After squaring the canvas, you draw, using dilute raw umber oil paint, then you establish the broad areas with more of the same. Then increase the tonal range with darker earth colours and highlight with white. Paint in the black and white areas first, the man's coat, his sleeve and flat square collar, the woman's collar, the greyish-blue marble tiles, the back wall, the dark-blue tiles. You block out the strongest areas of colour, the red of her tunic, her underdress, the blue chair in the middle ground. For the bluish dark tiles lay down bone black (it's actually brownish-looking); for the greyish marbled tiles, lay down lead white with some bone black and natural ultramarine; for the wall use lead white, azurite and bone black, for the window area, lead white and bone black. Of course, these are relatively general guidelines.

It hangs at the end of the corridor. If you turn left, you go into my studio, which gives onto the comfortable torture of a south London back garden, surmounted by clouds held in position like silver airships looking perversely heavy. If you turn right you're in the lighter, south-facing room, a kind of mini exhibition space. It has a sofa, and a piano that Sophie used to play.

'John . . .'

'Sophie? Where are you, for Christ's sake?'

'I don't know where I am, exactly. But there's a message: they want you to come to Delft. That's all I can say now.'

'When?'

'They'll let you know, soon.'

'Are you OK?'

'Yes, I'm OK, darling. Don't worry about me.'

## The Dance of Geometry

The flat is sparse. The main room looks out onto a wide, tree-lined canal. She's pretending not to register my incredulity that I should be here, with her, in her flat after one meeting.

'Shall we eat before or after?'

'The sketch?'

Only a smile, and she takes my arm and leads me to another room.

Her limbs are pale and thin but well-proportioned, like a Pinocchio doll. A very sexy, supple Pinocchio doll. But her eyes are not lying.

After the lovemaking, I hold on to those limbs, kneading them, confirming their contours in both hands. I have to tell her.

'I have plans, you know. I can't stay.'

'I know. I'll wait for you.'

'How long?' I queried.

I did other things for a living. Commissioned copies don't bring in enough, and with Sophie's looks . . . They knew, of course, though it did not occur to me at the time.

Sometimes we used the front room upstairs, sometimes the bedroom. I tried to get the whole as symmetrical, as square as possible, her arms extended at the ends of the ropes, her legs tapering down around a pole. Later she was floating in the air on a plane at an angle of about 30 degrees.

### The Mirror

You have outlined the ebony frame. Now you've got to imagine what will fill it before its counterpart takes its rightful place. She is turned towards him, exposing a three-quarter view of her face and shoulders. That's how she will stay, whatever happens from now on. He, waiting on her reply, is well-dressed, dignified, but you cannot say he is confident. He does not show his feelings easily, and neither does she (does anybody?). But then, of course, he is not there yet. The surface of the mirror is a little out of focus, as it should be. You cannot focus on both the content of the frame and its surroundings at the same time. I know this. Did *he?*

His women are all, in one way or another, captured, pinned down, squared off, enclosed, at the centre point of converging lines.

Sophie had a cousin living in Dresden. That was the only way I was going to get into that city and the gallery, *circa* 1987.

## The Ascending Leaves of the Painter, Johannes Vermeer of Delft

Not the laurel leaves on her thorny crown, nor their duplicate on the spectral canvas that seems to merge perfectly with the wall behind. No, those on the curtain that swirl upward with it and shade from light blue to dark, separated from the figure of the woman on the curtain whose shift duplicates and reverses the colour scheme of the model's dress. (Have I mentioned this before?) But what of the leaves themselves, which are blue? I will tell you that that is from oxidisation; they were green, of course, originally. One thing combines with two others, separates them and changes them forever. But the question is: What do you reproduce? The original green, for which there is no direct example, or how it is now? Which is truer? That you will have to decide for yourself.

*The Dance of Geometry*

## *Delft (again), The Go-Between*

I met K. in a pub off the old Beestenmarkt. We drank Duvel. He had the air of someone who had found the secret formula to a new rejuvenating product and was now sounding out the market. But he wanted to convince me. He was, as far as I could tell, a family man to whom comfort and security were paramount, yet for whom these meant nothing without a living passion.

This man knew not only where Vermeer had lived, but what he ate; not just what colours he used, but where he obtained them; not just how much his idol's paintings were worth, but who had been the owners through the years and how much had been paid for them. Of course, he did not just know these things as I knew them from checking my copious sources; he had an instinctive feeling born of his profession (he was an archaeologist) and of living in and treading the streets of Delft his whole life. He was Dutch, too, and I envied him for that alone. The main person who had to be convinced was himself and once that person had been won over, anyone listening to him would follow suit.

'I have been contacted,' he said.

'They want to make a deal?'

'They want a copy, for their purposes, no questions asked, no funny business with Marks and Spencer knickers under the corset, if you know what I mean?'

'So they want a fake. I don't do fakes.'

'You want Sophie back, surely? After all, who got you into this mess?'

'If I do this, that will be the end of it? The only one.'

'I cannot speak for them in every detail. When you meet with them, that will be the time to go over such matters.'

'I'll do a copy. You can call it what you like.'

'When will you have it ready?'
'In a month.'
'You work quickly. That is good. We will call you, Mr Lake.'

*One thing combines with two others, separates them and changes them forever.*

So I am either supposed to give her up—no tricks involved, no disclaimer hidden under the layers of paint—or I am to incriminate myself after all. They are forcing me to become a faker—in order to be true to the one person who has ever meant anything to me. Except I can't be sure if I won't be tricked at the last moment.

It would be ironic indeed if everything ended like that, when I have made a career out of copying artists who were past masters of trompe l'oeil, tricksters themselves. Perhaps I have been deceiving myself all along. Perhaps it's the price for not being original. Yet I can use my imagination.

*I am a smile now, fixed and framed, happy despite what you might think, and I believe I shall enjoy my new home. The view that I have may sometimes be familiar to you and may sometimes change; the view of me you will certainly know. But I shall make it clear for you nevertheless. My face is reflected in a mirror. The mirror is in the top half of the painting on the back wall above the virginal and, if I look up slightly, I can see myself playing at it. I would seem to be concentrating on the keyboards if you are looking from the back, yet as my face is reflected you would believe that my attention is more turned to the gentleman to my side. He is elegantly dressed, in a black coat, around which is draped a grey sash. His white shirtsleeves and his collar are very prominent, and he stands upright, with a cane in his left hand, upon which he lightly leans. Oh, he is pensive indeed. What he is and what he wishes to say,*

*The Dance of Geometry*

*the things that are left unsaid—these things are in my Master's mind and I do not know them.*

*I cannot move, it is true, but I can look and I can go back in my memory, and I am indeed taken forward, carried from one room or house at my owner's whim. I sometimes feel a deep yearning to see my own true self as I once used to see it when I looked up at my image in the mirror, but in many ways my life is richer. I study my different owners' faces, I see them grow older, become drunk, I see their joys and disappointments, their greed, and, usually, if they stay in possession of me long enough, I see them come to a new knowledge of themselves. But I am running ahead of myself. We must stay with the matter at hand.*

*I was brought to the household of Johannes Vermeer from Amsterdam by the painter's wealthy patron, as I later found out. It is strange, but I saw more of Johannes' work at Van Ruijven's than in the artist's own home. There I saw the sleeping maid, the view across the town from the Kolk, the maid pouring milk, the view of the street, the soldier passing a coin into the hand of a woman who could be bought, a woman drinking a glass of wine, a girl standing at a window reading a letter, and many others. I recall walking around Mijn Heer Van Ruijven's room and sometimes thinking that the figures were talking to me, beckoning me in. I told myself I was of lowly birth and unworthy of their company.*

*'You should not hold yourself in such low esteem,' Van Ruijven said on that first evening. He was standing against a very large, ornate mirror in the main room. He was a cold man and he did not seem to want me for my body, but my appearance was important to him.*

*'This man is a genius, but he is slow. I don't think I shall ever get back my money should I ever try to sell his works,' he said, 'though I cannot imagine ever doing that. Rather, I want more.'*

*I did not say anything in reply. He looked at me as if suddenly disappointed.*

'But why should I expect you to know or be interested in any of this? My wish is merely to make you pretty.'

And I thought that was true. He had taken pity on a woman of easy virtue who had had the fortune to work in an inn frequented by artists and art lovers. I know now, of course, more about art than I ever did before, having seen generations of them handle me. Of course, in more recent times I have been in the company of Queen Elizabeth of England herself. Yet despite these . . . distractions, my mind and heart are still in Holland.

I shall never forget the baths I was first given by Van Ruijven's maid and the clothes that I was told to wear—chemises, bodices, jackets of satin or taffeta, clothes that would have cost a half year's work (had I sought to go about such work honestly). And the food, especially the lobster and the wine in glasses so delicate I was afraid to handle them.

'You will model for him, that is all. You will be paid handsomely, of course. As I have said, he works slowly. You will be at his service for many months.'

Now somebody enters the room. It is her, his wife. She looks up at me as if in triumph. Oh, how she would like to obliterate me, erase all my features, features that she dearly loves to pretend to herself to be her own, but she cannot. The work is intended for Mijn Heer Van Ruijven. Many times she will come to his house. To gloat? To plot a rescue, to make my captivity complete? She would not buy it back, surely and hire someone to . . . No, she does not have the money. Besides, another painting is more precious to her and her shrewish mother.

She looks now to her right, as if to speak to someone whom I cannot see. Or is she sad at my death?

'Johannes, you will sell this painting?'

'It is sold. To Van Ruijven.'

'Then where is the money?'

'It will come, do not worry.'

*'He has now many paintings of ours...'*

*She says: 'of ours.' The presumption of that woman!*

*'You need not be afraid.'*

*He is unwilling to confront her. Tell her the truth, Johannes. Yet I know you cannot.*

*'You are gloomy, since...'*

*Since my death. Say it.*

*'I am thinking of the future, with another baby...'*

*'That is why I mentioned the money.'*

*'What do you expect me to do except work? That is where my thoughts lie now.'*


It is the first day. He begins with the mirror. The drawing is already there, the design is clear to me. I stand facing the glass in full costume, and he works, saying nothing. I hear the sound of the market sellers from the Great Market Square and the bells of the Nieuwe Kerk pealing. It is noisier than some parts of Amsterdam on a day like this. His children run along the corridor screaming and then suddenly stop. I know that they are looking through the keyhole. I can hear their whispers, but Mijn Heer Vermeer, who I can sometimes see in the mirror, shows no irritation. Oh, but he works so slowly!

To my right, I can see a most valuable painting of an old man with his hands chained behind his back sucking at the breast of a young woman. I do not know who they are but I am certain that they must be important people in history, for else it would be indecent. In the inn in Amsterdam, there were many pictures of dogs engaging in the act or a soldier touching a woman in a private place. You could not imagine the like in this place. Yet I believe this painting, like most in the house, belongs to Mijn Heer Vermeer's mother-in-law.

'You should imagine a gentleman to your right,' he says. 'Turn your head a little in that direction.'

*He said imagine, but I did not have to do so for long, for, whenever Mijn Heer van Ruijven could not attend, an elegant gentleman by the name of Constantijn Huygens would come to visit on these occasions. He had offered to pose (for he was the same height as Mijn Heer van Ruijven), something, which like myself, he was not experienced in. But he held conversations with Mijn Heer Vermeer, and sometimes disappeared with him into the room from which Mijn Heer Vermeer worked and that I was not permitted to enter. Yet on those occasions that he was concentrated on his task of posing, he did this with such application that I was quite disconcerted, for I was, naturally, the object of his gaze. Mijn Heer van Ruijven, on the other hand, showed little interest in the dark room.*

*But some days we were completely alone, and Mijn Heer Vermeer showed a strong interest in me.*

'You are from Amsterdam, Maritje?'

'Yes, sir.'

'This is your first time, to model, I think?'

'Yes, sir.'

'You may speak with more words than just "Yes, sir", you understand.'

*I felt my shyness thawing, particularly when I noticed that a small smile played about his lips, as if he would like to continue teasing me, but was holding himself back.*

'Mijn Heer van Ruijven has taken you under his wing, we could say?'

'Sir, I do not think I am at liberty to speak of my guardian . . .'

'Guardian?'

'He calls himself my guardian, though legally it is not so.'

'Yes, I should wonder at what his wife says to that.'

'I would like to know about your painting . . .'

'You are direct, if nothing else.'

'Nothing else? Am I not pleasing in your eyes?'

'You may be pretty but vain with it to ask such a question.'

'Sir, please do not be offended. I . . . should like to know more. I have seen many of your paintings, and . . .'

'And . . .'

'They are most wonderful, I think.'

'Who bade you speak like that? Van Ruijven? He is cunning indeed.'

'Oh, no, he is genuine, most genuine. He wants me to speak as a lady.'

'But did he not find you in . . . a brothel . . . ?'

'Mijn Heer, he merely visited the inn where I worked, and took pity on me.'

'No doubt. In any case, it is enough for today.'

'But sir . . .' I said these last words fearing I had estranged myself from this man, so abrupt was the conclusion to this meeting.

Back to the drawing board, or canvas, as it were. So you want to copy? But you also want to relive, to re-enact. That means: START AGAIN! Get into the atmosphere of the whole thing. You've got to recreate that room, down to the most minute detail. Now that will be as hard as it sounds, if you take that literally. Not only do you have to find a reasonable substitution for a virginal and marble tiles, a room with two or three bays of windows facing north (not forgetting that they have mullions), a vintage mirror, and a copy of a *Roman Charity*. You'll also have to find a reasonable set of authentic clothing, a recording of the kind of music that would have been played at the time (we'll take a guess here at what Maritje is playing; Bach is a safe bet). Did Jan, (or V., as I prefer to think of him), in fact insist that his model play the virginal? Was he like Stanley Kubrick, demanding a hundred takes (or poses) for the simplest pieces? The parallel isn't as fanciful as it might seem—when you consider how few works V. probably produced in his lifetime, even allowing for a certain percentage that haven't survived. He must have been a stickler for detail, working extremely slowly.

Now this calls for rethinking. Or Stage Two. It's well known that Jan almost certainly couldn't have owned his own virginal, given his means, despite the fact that, around this time, they were fair and consistently improving. But he still would never have had enough to buy one of these. He could conceivably have borrowed one, but it is more likely that he simply drew sketches from an instrument belonging to someone more likely to have possessed one locally, such as Van Ruijven or even Huygens himself. Who was the more likely to have had one? My money is on Van Ruijven. So, if we work under the assumption that Vermeer probably didn't have a virginal in his studio, it's possible that he didn't have other things or at least that they weren't necessarily all present in the relative proximity to each other in which you see them in the paintings. An obvious statement to some, perhaps. But consider the tiles, for example, which appear in different patterns and with different designs and colours throughout his work in what appears to be the same room or studio. Ah, a breath of fresh air. Conclusion: Vermeer took liberties, as may any artist worthy of the name. Ergo, we may do the same.

Let's start with using a recording for the virginal playing. We can find a table carpet from Turkey of a similar colour scheme and design; the mirror won't pose too many problems, though the size is important. The viola da gamba is a cinch. The windows, ceiling coffers and virginal are another matter, but, as with the master, we shall simply have to find these objects, make our own sketches, and project them onto our studio. As for the costumes, well, we can rent them. Now, that's better.

Of course, I have to be careful here not to get sidetracked by my multiple-purpose narrative. I am trying to instruct readers of this manual, and for that I presume you have time, all the time in the world, but I've got just one month, and, like the best television cook, I've had the foresight to get most of the ingredients together. In fact, I have not been completely straight with you. I could have told you we should do all this from the start. Perhaps you simply imagined the conditions, assumed that this entire atmosphere was already there. Well, now you can rest assured that it is in place, even down to my copy of the *Roman Charity* (the original for this painting within *The Music Lesson* itself may have been by Christiaen van Couwenbergh—unless *that* was a copy).

What is missing is some of the research, research into costumes of the period, into music of the period, carpet-making, manners, even the inscription on the upturned lid of the instrument. Not forgetting knowing something about the rest of Vermeer's oeuvre, that of his contemporaries, the local history of Delft and Dutch history of the time. I've prepared this, but should you take it on yourself to copy this painting or any other for that matter, you will have to do the legwork yourself.

Now, you are not expected to use your wife or girlfriend as the model, nor will it be asked of you to provide the CIA with a copy that is going to be used in a sting operation that is going to endanger you and your family . . . quite apart from bankrupting you. That is taking verisimilitude too far—in so far as our Jan was virtually bankrupt by the time of his death. Although, by all means, do whatever you need to get you in the mood. Maybe I shouldn't be so cynical.

### *Technique*

There is one more area where you could, and this is speculative, increase the authenticity of this particular project: by considering how the artist achieved the effects he did. One theory is that he used a camera obscura, or a darkroom, where he traced the outline of the studio scene to achieve that particularly tricky, slightly distorted perspective that is so outstanding in the painting. It would also have contributed to the intensity of colour that is not unalloyed to the kind witnessed when you see such an image with this device. As an alternative to this, or possibly an additional means of preparation, there is the possibility that he drew so-called distance points to either side of the canvas on the horizon line (which you have to determine, since it is variable), to which he attached pins. From these pins he hung and stretched two short pieces of string covered in chalk, which he snapped against the canvas at various intervals. Where they crossed and where they met with an additional piece of string hung from the dead centre of the horizon line, this would have produced the eye-catching tile pattern that grounded the perspective of the picture.

Another way to get into the period would be to try to recreate and relive some dramatic moments from Vermeer's life, a short story perhaps, but I think that that is above and beyond the call of duty; besides which, its feasibility is rather dubious.

They will not have *my* copy. They will have another. They will have their true fake—if they so desire.

[How to get that subtle shift of blue in the tiles. They start off grey-black at the back of the room and proceed to a fuller dark blue in the foreground . . . ]

It's strange to find myself back in south London after all this time, that I should choose to live here, where I grew up. When I was growing up, I could only think of travelling away, across Europe, a longing inspired by my facility with languages. I think of it as a historical mistake that I excelled at German—I should have been taught Dutch in the first place. Then the university years, Austria and Germany, back to London, then further tours, this time with a sketchpad in hand.

## The Dance of Geometry

I often think that my childhood wasn't so unlike Vermeer's. A working-class childhood, a simple but hard-working father, short but threateningly strong. He was once threatened by a neighbour and my sister and mother had to wrestle with him while he waved around a flick-knife I had never seen before. I was five at the time.

In school, I made my way up the helpful ladder of comprehensive education, with a lot of encouragement; my mother coached me, my sister comforted me. I couldn't decide if I should become an artist or a linguist—they were two sides of the same coin for me. Then, somewhere along the way, I lost the courage. I got sidetracked into copying others. I came under the influence of indisputable masters, and one in particular. But you don't want to hear a hard luck story. You want to have your own painting.

For the darkroom all you'll need are the heavy, dark curtains in which you have cut a small hole. Providing the rest of the room is sealed against light, you will get an image of the outside world on the wall. To apply this method to your studio, you will have to construct a small room at the back of the studio whose wall contains a small hole. Whatever you put in that room will shine through that aperture onto the inner back wall of your darkroom. The image will be inverted, and reversed laterally, of course—unless you can devise a way to cut a hatch-like opening into that far wall, which you will cover with tracing paper. On the other side you can then trace a positive image of the scene.

You're about ready to start, if all these things are in place. I certainly am, and now I have to escort my beauty to the rendezvous point.

*I returned to Mijn Heer van Ruijvens's house as soon as I had been dismissed. He was eager to know about the progress of the work. I was fed handsomely, and engaged in conversation with my Master until light faded from the street outside. The room in which we often sat was quite dark. I had, not for the first time, the sensation that my Master was studying my face as if its features were already committed to canvas, and I felt sometimes that I was locked under the coat of oil and varnish that are now so familiar to me, at the mercy of his gaze. Yet, strangely, it was not an unpleasant feeling. And during that time, my knowledge grew, beyond all reasonable expectations.*

*Mijn Heer van Ruijven took it upon himself to teach me to read, to fill my head with all the new knowledge, which was flooding Holland. Yes, there is no better word for it, flooding, despite the inappropriateness of such a choice of word.*

*Right now I am being viewed in a gallery in London by a young man whose gaze reminds me of Mijn Heer van Ruijven. This man will go on to fall dramatically in love, I feel sure. He has that look, the look of a man who can be mesmerised by a painted image, a pretty face, giving everything for it. It is now the year 1989 but I have seen that look on many occasions, and in every century, since that time—in Holland, in England, in Italy, a country whose atmosphere I miss so much. Johannes, it is a place you would have loved indeed. I feel regret that you could never know such places yourself.*

Yes, it was the coincidence that did it for me. *The Music Lesson* is not an easy painting to find, even if you call the Royal Collection. But in 1989 my luck was in, and I had an appointment with it that would not be delayed at any cost. You could find it in The Queen's Gallery at the back of the Palace. I took up unofficial residence in front of the painting. Nothing prepares you for the reality of that work. Firstly, it's lighter and bluer than most colour reproductions.

Five years earlier I had been in love with Sophie but we had broken up over some small misunderstanding. We hadn't been in contact all that time. Yet when I found myself looking in the mirror that reflected only the inner space of the painting's world, I felt sure I was seeing another reflection there. A turn of the head a moment later, a little deeper absorption, and I wouldn't ever have known.

As I turn round, I'm looking at Sophie. She has barely changed. Except that she's wearing glasses. I have forgotten that her eyes are so narrow; her features seem squeezed into higher definition. Her posture is erect. She must have been modelling all this time. No words pass between us for an inhuman amount of time. She moves away. No, it can't be. But that's Sophie, I tell myself. And I'm caught. This is the last day of the exhibition. Well, I know I'm a chronic procrastinator, but I have no good excuses for this. I have to make a choice; I have to leave one past image behind to retrieve another in life, before me.

And that's how it started again.

*Dark boxes, dark boxes. That is their obsession. What am I but an image to them? No, that is not how I feel. But Johannes, you spent so much time away from me, there, in your dark room.*

*I am not allowed to turn. I can wear this beautiful bodice and skirt, but they are hard, like your demands. All I see of you, thanks to the mirror, is that small hole in the wood there at the back of the room for hours on end. Is it good for your eyes, even? Let me see you now. And occasionally,* she *comes into the room and looks around; satisfied, perhaps, not to find us in there together. Then there are your children, or sometimes it is an illustrious guest. In particular there was that over-excited, obsequious French gentleman, Mon-something. He was looking for a mystery, I think. And he certainly got it.*

*Ah, I see what you are doing now. Now I remember the beginnings.*

*You have finally completed the drawing. It's all there, the mirror, the virginal, the carpet, the painting, the gentleman, the windows, the tiles, the vase, the ceiling coffers. Now all that remains is for him to put me in this setting. Now you are taking the oiled paper and turning it upside down, you are placing it on the canvas on the bench.*

## Another method

Inside the darkroom you trace the outline of the scene onto the paper. You prick the design, making a number of evenly spaced pinpricks through the drawing onto the canvas beneath. You take some pounce (powdered charcoal) and sprinkle it over the little holes. Lift the sheet up, and there on the canvas you have your scene. That is one method. Now go back to '*Ground*'.

You will need a 'colour balanced'[4] light box for the colour transparency, if you can get your hands on one, as well as a good black-and-white photograph of the original. The latter will give you a better tonal range than a colour photograph. If you are following the camera obscura method, you will only be using the above for reference, but if that is beyond you, you will need an actual-size photograph (black-and-white or colour) of part of the painting taken in 'raking' light—the common technique by which the surface details of a painting are revealed by light cast across it at a low angle.

Over this photographic detail place two canvases, one raw, one primed, in order to judge the 'tooth' or type of weave closest to the original canvas. The best unbleached flax canvases can be obtained from Ireland and Belgium these days. Then square up a photograph, drawing onto the canvas with a pencil.

*The now familiar outline comes through again, like sand blown across the beach to reveal a buried person: all of the above, me, Maritje and Mijn Heer van Ruijven, who any moment might indeed walk in. And, as I remember, that is what happened.*

'Ah, Johannes, Maritje,' he dips his head slightly to acknowledge me, and, seeing the traced image on the empty canvas, says, 'curious, curious'.

'Pieter van Ruijven, you have seen this method many times before,' replies Johannes.

'Oh, really. I don't recall.' And he winks at me.

'What is the purpose of such an early visit, Pieter?'

'Ah, about the gentleman. It should be me, do you not think?'

Johannes laughs in an abrupt, mirthless way. He does not look pleased. What is he thinking? He had intended to paint a hidden portrait of himself and Catharina, but now he has me in the mirror with Mijn Heer van Ruijven. Husband and wife have turned into guardian and ward, or probably father and daughter, if he could have his way. No, I don't think he will be pleased.

'How do you create this effect, Johannes?'

'In there.' Johannes points generally at the wooden wall.

'Where?'

'You cannot see it?'

Mijn Heer van Ruijven walks over to the partition and moves a hand over it as if looking for a hidden door. As he does so, he notices, at eye level, the small hole inset with the glass. He is about to probe it with his finger, when Johannes shouts, 'No, leave that, Pieter.'

Abruptly, as if to distract van Ruijven's attention from the delicate lens, Johannes pulls on a small ribbon, which makes a light door swing open, and they go in together.

'Maritje,' he calls to me, 'stand at the virginal, please.'

They are in there for perhaps a half hour. I can only hear the low voices in an excited, muffled discussion. When they emerge, Van Ruijven looks flustered, excited in a way I have never seen him before. Johannes looks distracted. He is not certain whether he has been visited by fortune or disaster, I think.

*In the mirror (I have not turned round) Mijn Heer van Ruijven comes over to me. At first I think that he will accompany me out, but instead of taking my arm, he takes up a position to my right, his left hand resting on his cane. He is wearing a long black coat, with a square, white flat collar. The ruffed collars of his shirt are bright white too, and he is wearing a pinkish sash. I turn to face him for a moment, his gaze level with mine.*

*'Turn to the mirror, Maritje.'*

*I do so, and, as I do, my gaze falls on the Latin inscription on the lid of the virginal.*

*'What does it mean, sir?' I say.*

*'Maritje, do not worry yourself about such things now.'*

*'I mean the writing, sir, here.'*

*'Ah, music indeed. The companion of joy, the medicine of sadness.'*

*'You are not sad, I hope?'*

*'No, no, far from it, Maritje. Far from it.'*

One thing combines with two others, separates them and changes them forever. One thing, one person, it is true.

### The Frame

I would go for a period frame. Leave it in the hands of a frame maker; give him the dimensions, a rough outline of what kind you need, plain wood or possibly one of the gilt, auricular types. For plentiful examples of the former you only have to look at some of the paintings (or even the mirrors) within V.'s own works. I favour the plain ebony kind that you actually see surrounding the mirror in *The Music Lesson* itself.

The call comes right on time, at the end of the calendar month.

'They're going to come to you.' It's K.

'What about Sophie?'
'You'll see her in time.'
'Have *you* seen her?'
'Yes, don't worry.'
'When are they coming?'
'Soon. Don't go anywhere, not even to the shops.'

He's gone before I can delay him any further. I wanted to tell him it's going to be quite a while before the paint is hard and it can be varnished, but what the hell.

At least there'll be no smuggling over borders for me. But I'm a sitting duck, from now on in, I know.

I'm assuming that they'll double/triple/quadruple-cross me, of course, take the picture, kill me, kill Sophie, maybe even kill K. Technically, I've broken the law anyway with this copy. They know where I am, and I'm not going anywhere. So, they'll have it, the painting that is, but I won't be there for them, not in person.

*From the window of the room where I was housed in Venice for some years I could see the deceptive emerald green depths of the water. With no sun shining, it is a dark sludge-like green, but at a certain angle it goes from emerald to turquoise to cerulean. From where do I know such words, you ask. Why, from the lords and ladies of the embassy here who pass by me, smiling at me as if I were their queen.*

*Now I am surrounded by a gilt frame. I do not know if I like it so much. It is ill fitting, like a heavy coat on a summer's day. And this consul, Joseph Smith, would take us for the work of Frans van Mieris. Huh!*

*How long is it now since that day when Johannes realised Van Ruijven's intentions? Was it so terrible that his patron should demand that he and I should be more than just models, that Van Ruijven should want the painting as his portrait? An unusual definition of a portrait, to be sure. Why, Johannes, wasn't this painting supposed to be dedicated to your wife?*

**Girl Reading a Letter at an Open Window**, *c*. 1657, 83 x 64.5 cm.

We went there together, twice. The first time was on the way back to England. She had a cousin who belonged to the side of her family that had found itself living in East Germany. They got me in by having her cousin write a letter inviting me to stay there for a few days. The Zwinger Museum was still the Zwinger, and the Vermeers (they have two) were still Vermeers, if a little in need of a clean. I knew that after this trip we weren't going to be able to see each other for some time, if at all. It was 1983, and how could I have known that this painting would chart the course of the next six years, in which I would keep hanging on to her image?

I don't have any time to lose, so follow me quickly into my pre-prepared darkroom. It's narrow, and the entrance door is disguised. I am banking on them being fooled. Too much to hope that they will appreciate the irony? Probably. But there is still a chance they will leave me—us—alone. The only thing that might give me away is the small lens in the partition.

I put the painting on the easel, pretty much in the style of *The Art of Painting*. Next to it, on a small worktable, I place a letter. You might never know what it says. Maybe something like:

'Here's your bloody painting. Now leave me alone.'

Maybe it's a message for her, saying, I shall always love you etc., etc. After which, I shall pop out of my little room like a jack-in-a-box, we'll embrace, kiss, and it'll all be over. Whatever happens, I'll be able to see them on the circular screen projected

## The Dance of Geometry

onto the back wall, unless they come after sunset. Then I won't be able to view them in this true camera obscura style. I will be reduced to just using the lens as a peephole.

The light is still streaming in from the left and it's getting very stuffy in here when I hear the front-door bell ring. Well, I'm not about to answer it, and if it's them, I won't need to. A few more rings, then silence. I think I hear scratching at some surface, then the tread of feet. One, two pairs of feet. Up the short flight of stairs. An arm scuffs the side of the wall as one of them goes straight to the studio. He must be quite light, not the bulky job you'd expect, and the other must have stayed back or gone into another room.

A ghostly figure walks into the room, blotting out the canvas. Sophie! I want to blurt out but it's too dangerous. She picks up the letter on the table and stands reading it, the light almost drowning her out. She stands there like a statue while the floorboards creak from the steps of her unseen companion. He must be rummaging around the rest of the house.

Finally, he appears, uncertainly, doesn't at first notice the painting, just looks at her reading the letter. Now he sees the canvas, his eyes registering rapid admiration. A glance is enough. He turns slightly. Enough for me to see that it is K. and he is holding a gun. He takes the damned thing, seems on the point of saying something to Sophie, puts his arms around her waist, (and I hold my breath in horror, thinking this is his tender prelude to putting the gun to her temple). K. holds her in a way that would never have been tolerated in Johannes' household, but, to my relief and utter dismay, her hands come up willingly to clasp around his neck. Sophie turns to look at the back wall. She looks straight back at me. She knows.

## Notes

1 *Johannes Vermeer*, A. K. Wheelock, ed, catalogue of an exhibition in Washington and The Hague, November 1995–June 1996; National Gallery of Art, Washington, Royal Cabinet of Paintings, Mauritshuis, The Hague, and Yale University Press, New Haven & London, 1995.

2 'Ground' when referring to a painting is a rather ambiguous term. It can mean just the first, priming layers of paint and oil on the canvas which prevent the oil paints sinking into and rotting the canvas itself and which also give the painting depth and tone, or it can mean everything from the wooden support, the canvas, the priming, up to the imprimatura layers. *I* use it strictly in the former sense.

3 Made from rabbit skin, in bags of crystals. Not for the squeamish, and mind that smell!

4 The colour of the light that shines through the transparency is as close to daylight as possible (5000 Kelvin, that is).

# Part four:
## *The Shifting Surface of Desire (reprise)*

Catharina climbs the stairs, passing on the way a series of paintings by her husband and his peers. Why had he not sold these works? They would surely fetch sums above the average if he died? She crosses herself, then manoeuvres her still shapely form, encumbered as she is by layers of fresh blankets, into the room where her eldest daughter has been keeping watch.

He could see now the brittleness of her smile, yes, a smile that fissured as if to anticipate the radial craquelure that would eventually come to his painting. He waved for some water and his daughter Maria walked over to the angled window, open to dispel the room's mustiness, and poured some into his glass. Something here in his daughter's concentration recalled the inspiration for that image so long stored away under the surface of oil and varnish that he had almost forgotten the source. But here she was again, her features superimposed upon his daughter's, as if the very canvas were being held up to him.

On his deathbed, Monsignor Johannes Vermeer was capable of little communication; light was once more everything. The smile returned to the face of his eldest daughter and to that of his wife. Downstairs, his offspring ran about the house, their limbs powered by blood he had given them, making a pulsing map out of lives to come. The final note was not dulling, but a white flash, as if pulling aside a curtain protecting a picture. And again it was the smile, but this time there was no doubt, no dissimulation.

# Some of the terms . . .

**Amorum Emblemata**   1608, a book of engravings by Otto van Veen

**astrolabe**   an instrument formerly used to take altitudes and to solve other astronomical problems

**camera obscura**   a dark room with a small aperture admitting sunlight and a white sheet serving as a projection screen, which imparts a strange, almost magical kind of movement to objects and people. The effect is a lot like watching a movie nowadays

**cartouches**   tiny rectangular scenes that run around the edges of the larger painting as in Vermeer's *The Art of Painting*

**chaconne**   (1685, OED) 'an obsolete dance, the music to which it was danced, moderately slow'

**clavecin**   the French term for the what the English called a 'virginal'—an instrument where the strings are stretched parallel to the keyboard, whereas, in a harpshichord, they are at right angles to it. Art critics concur that the instrument in *The Music Lesson* was a clavecin or virginal.

**conclave**   a religious gathering or clandestine meeting

**the Kolk**   the triangular harbour on a slip of land in the south of Delft from which Vermeer is universally believed to have painted *A View of Delft*

**kermis**  a periodical fair or carnival, characterised by much noisy merrymaking

**kolf**  a game on the ice, similar to ice-hockey. The fight on the ice with kolf (hockey) sticks in which Reynier is involved is a deliberate conflation of two incidents, as retailed in Montias, with which Vermeer's father was actually associated. The first of these was a fight between Reynier, two friends, and an army captain in 1625. (Though an amicable agreement was reached, the captain later died from his injuries.) The second incident, a decade later, in 1635, involved Reynier and his work colleagues, who intervened in a fight on the ice between another colleague and a man.

**musico**  a term for taverns of the kind where people had a good time and music was played

**predikant**  a minister in the Dutch Protestant Church

**putto, putti**  representations of toddler-aged children, either nude or in swaddling bands, 15th–17th century Italy

**Prinsenhof**  a complex of buildings in Delft, formerly a sixteenth-century convent, in the hands of the States of Holland, where Prince William of Orange had been assassinated (1584). In Vermeer's time it 'was used for various representative purposes,' so it is the sort of illustrious building that notables might gather in and would be suitably labyrinthine. The hall that the assembly eventually uses might even be the famous great or large hall, which, a few years later, Bramer would decorate with murals on the ceiling and wall.

**raking light**  a term meaning a technique for revealing surface details of a painting by casting light across it at a low angle

**rules of parallax**  the apparent change in the position of an object resulting from a change in the position of the observer

**voorhuis**  the large entrance hall of a Dutch home

# Some of the Personages...

**Aelst, Evert van** (1602–1657)—minor still life painter, uncle and master of the more famous Willem, was well-known in Delft for his works in the 'modern' style of the 1640s.

**Ast, Balthasar van der** (1590–1660)—moving to Delft in midlife, (1632), Van der Ast was highly regarded for his elaborate, precisely-painted groupings of flowers and seashells.

**Bloemaert, Abraham** (1564–1651)—a distant relative of Vermeer's mother-in-law, Maria Thins, the Catholic Bloemaert was the leading member of the Utrecht Mannerist school. It is thought that he might have taught Vermeer at some point during the young painter's apprenticeship. Maria Thins herself owned a modest collection of Utrecht paintings (of which the *Roman Charity* depicted within *The Music Lesson* is one example).

**Bramer, Leonaert** (1596–1674)—a Catholic artist, one of Vermeer's mentors; he was a prolific painter and draughtsman of principally biblical and mythological scenes. During the 1630s and 1640s he painted canvas murals for princely palaces. He was a highly respected member of the painters' guild, serving as headman in 1644–45, followed by two further terms in 1660, and 1664–65.

**Bres, Tobias** —captain in the army of the States-General, a military contractor, workmaster, friend and partner in various undertakings with Johannes' maternal uncle, Reynier Balthens. One of their projects led to a suit against them by an investor for failing satisfactorily to complete repairs to the ramparts of a fortified town wall around the town of Brouwershaven in 1652.

**Buyten, Hendrick van** —wealthy Delft baker who collected paintings as part-payment for the Vermeer family's very large bread debt; these included at least three Vermeer works. One of these was seen and commented on in his diaries by Monconys on one of the latter's visits to Delft.

**Couwenbergh, Christiaen van** (1604–1667)—Delft's leading history and genre painter of the 1630s and 1640s, whose international style was inspired by cosmopolitan painters such as Rubens, and whose own career underwent great fluctuations. He moved his family to The Hague to execute court commissions, but accumulated debts there and withdrew to Cologne at the end of his life.

**De Monconys, Balthasar** (1611–1665)—a learned, Jesuit-educated, French diplomat and connoisseur of art, particularly interested in modern Dutch painters. Accompanied by "Gentillo' and Père Léon, he visited Vermeer in August, 1663. He had been referred to him by Constantijn Huygens, who was amazed to learn that De Monconys had been in the city the previous week and visited the tomb of William the Silent but not Vermeer's studio. De Monconys was to make two more visits to Delft in the next eight days before he would meet the painter.

**Dou, Gerard** (1613–1675)—a former pupil of Rembrandt, Dou went on to become the founder of the Leiden school of *fijnschilders* (fine painters) and one of the most famous Dutch genre painters of the seventeenth century. Dou's paintings were prized for their meticulous technique and attention to detail.

**Dürer, Albrecht** (1471–1528)—painter, engraver and most influential artist of the German School. Dürer is known for his technical mastery, his theoretical contributions and his adoption of the principles of the Italian Renaissance.

**Fabritius, Carel** —long considered one of Rembrandt's most gifted disciples and precursor of Vermeer. Along with Van Hoogstraten, he was one of the premier illusionistic painters of this period; he was born in 1622 and died when he was only 33, in the Delft arsenal explosion.

**Fornenburgh, Jan Baptist van** (*c.*1585–1648)—accomplished flower painter, linked to Vermeer through the latter's father, Reynier Vermeer, who had provided lodgings for the painter's soldier son Barend, in 1631, before Barend left for the Dutch East Indies, where he was later killed. In 1640 Reynier Vermeer also acted as witness when Van Fornenburgh came to Delft to collect his son's back pay.

**Gentillo, Lieutenant-Colonel** —this visitor of Vermeer's was only recently discovered to be Louis Cousin (1606–1667), a Catholic artist originally from Flanders who had enjoyed a long, successful career in Rome before settling and continuing to work in Brussels. He was known more commonly as Luigi Gentile.

**Groenewegen, Pieter Anthonisz. van** (*c.*1600–1658?)—a landscapist who had worked in Rome in his youth alongside Bramer. The son of wealthy parents, his works are cited often in Delft inventories and Vermeer's father, Reynier, dealt in them.

**Hondius, Hendrick** —printer and publisher, and one of the foremost admirers of De Vries, Hondius published several treatises on perspective (including De Vries' influential *Perspective*, 1604–5)

**Hooch, Pieter de** (1629–1684)—usually considered the second most important representative of the Delft School after Vermeer, although he lived in Delft for only a period of five years, in the late 1650s, at the end of which he moved to the flourishing art centre of Amsterdam. He is said to have died in an asylum for the insane.

**Hoogstraten, Samuel van** (1627–1678)—a fellow pupil of Carel Fabritius under Rembrandt. Theoretician and painter well-known for his illusionistic or trompe l'oeil paintings, murals, and for his perspective boxes (or peep shows). Lived in Dordrecht, Vienna, London, and The Hague. (During the novel's events he was probably in London, but authorial licence here has him make a brief trip to Delft).

**Huygens, Constantijn, the Elder** (1596–1687)—secretary and art advisor to the Dutch stadholders Frederick Hendrick and Willem II; he was the most influential arbiter of taste in The Hague.

**IMV** Ioannis, an earlier version of Johannis. The signature IVM is on nearly all of Vermeer's paintings.

**Langue, Willem de** —respected Delft notary and art collector who often represented artists. He was a friend of the Vermeers. His collection was reputed to have been substantial.

**Leeuwenhoek, Anthony van** (1632–1723)—born in Delft the same year as Vermeer, the self-educated Van Leeuwenhoek lived a long, productive life, working as a draper and civic official. He was a keen amateur scientist, and one of the first microbiologists, even constructing his own lenses and microscopes. (There is no proof that he and Vermeer actually met; however, Van Leeuwenhoek was given the task of executing Vermeer's estate.)

**Léon, Père** —commonly known as Leo Maes of Brussels, he accompanied De Monconys on the latter's third visit to Delft in 1663 on a visit to the city's Catholic neighborhood. He was a Carmelite priest, almoner of the French embassy, and a celebrated preacher in The Hague.

**Loo, Jacob van** (1614–1670)—Amsterdam painter and possible master of Vermeer. Progressed from large canvases with mythological or religious scenes to smaller genre scenes, including so-called Merry Companies or society pieces.

**Maes, Nicolaes** (1634–1693)—from Dordrecht, studied under Rembrandt, and specialised in rather charming genre pieces which employed illusionistic effects; his work was usually considered somewhat below the standard of the top rank of Delft painters with which he was associated in the 1650s. He may well have influenced De Hooch, and thereby Vermeer.

**Maurits, Prince** the eldest son of Willem the Silent, Maurits took over the throne at the age of seventeen when his father was assassinated in 1584. He later became the stadholder of Holland and Zeeland. A leading patron of the arts, during his reign he developed the importance of the sovereign's splendour and magnificence as a primary element in statesmanship.

**Neercassel, Hendrick Claesz. van** —a friend and colleague of Reynier Balthens, Johannes' maternal uncle. He took part in the successful siege of Sas van Gent in Flanders in 1644, helping Balthens construct the "left gallery" of the siege engine.

**Rietwijck, Cornelis Daemen** (1589–1660)—a Catholic portrait painter in the Delft Guild who ran a small academy in the Voldersgracht in 1641 and who may have instructed the young Johannes.

**Rijn, Rembrandt van** (1606–69)—master of the Dutch school and one of the great Western painters of all time. He produced some 600 paintings, including over 100 self-portraits, 300 etchings and 2,000 drawings—all distinguished by their profound humanity.

**Ripa, Cesare** —author of the *Iconologia* (Rome, 1603), which, in the Dutch translation by Dirck Pers (Amsterdam, 1644), had a substantial influence on the symbolism and imagery in Vermeer's paintings.

**Ruijven, Pieter Claesz. van** (1624–1674)—wealthy patrician and patron of Vermeer, he owned the largest number of Vermeer paintings.

**Terborch, Gerard** (1617–1681)—a specialist in elegant society or 'conversation pieces' (as well as a successful portraitist), he is credited with a number of innovations in this genre. He was particularly skilled at representing the sheen of satin and silk, and shared a number of motifs and themes with Vermeer. It has been mooted that he may have been present at Vermeer's wedding.

**Trakl, Georg** (1887–1914)—born in Salzburg, he was an expressionist poet and writer of fiction whose personal and wartime torments made him Austria's foremost elegist of decay and death. A pharmacist and later a lieutenant in the army medical corps in Galicia, he was responsible at one stage for 90 men, and witnessed so many horrors of war that he attempted suicide and later, he died of a cocaine overdose—possibly intentionally. His work had a large impact on German-language poetry after both world wars.

**Vignola, Giacomo Barozzi da** (1507–1573)—Italian painter and architect, whose treaty on perspective, *Le Due regole della* *prospettiva practica di M. Iacomo Barozzi da Vignola,* was published in 1583, and may well have been one of the texts available to Vermeer and other Dutch painters of the time.

**Vredeman de Vries, Hans** (1527–1607)—architect, designer and founding father of architectural painting in the Netherlands, he lived in The Hague and later in Hamburg. His legacy was kept alive by a number of Dutch artists and architects.

**Witte, Emanuel de** (1617–1692), contemporary of Vermeer who specialised in painting the interiors of churches.

# Acknowledgements

The genesis of this novel has been long and has taken many winding turns on its way. I hope that I am able to thank all those people and acknowledge the various sources I have consulted (listed below), but if I had to single out at least one person, it would be Leo Stevenson, who not only gave unstintingly of his help, advice and input, but added his invaluable knowledge and skills as an artist and all-round polymath. If I had to choose just one book, it would be *The Art of Describing* by Svetlana Alpers.

John Michael Montias' ground-breaking work, *Vermeer and His Milieu*, and Philip Steadman's earlier work on Vermeer's use of the camera obscura, particularly as it first appeared in an educational programme on British television, provided great inspiration. The extensive 1996 exhibition in The Hague, along with its indispensable ancillary exhibitions, proved an unexpected luxury which appeared on the horizon as I was halfway through this book.

I would like to thank the following people who have helped me during my research for this book: John Michael Montias,

*The Dance of Geometry*

Martin Kemp, Philip Steadman, Elizabeth de Bièvre, David Bomford, Jørgen Wadum, David Hockney, and Jeroen Kistemaker for help with technical information, discussion, and encouragement; Andrew Motion, Russell Celyn Jones, Janette Turner Hospital, Nicholas Royle, Richard Skinner, Phil Whitaker, Jai Clare, Jeff Edmunds, Kirsten Snipp, Oliver Baty, Meredith Allard, Philip Smith, Matthew Ryan, Anne Schaeffer, Rhys Williams and Aliki Varvogli all contributed editorial and general advice. And for their unceasing belief in this book, I would like to thank my publisher, Matthew Miller, my agent Giles Gordon, and my editor, Aloma Halter.

My thanks also to the editors of *Fishtank* (1996), in which an earlier version of the first section of this novel appeared, as well as to Meredith Allard, who also published an extract from the second section in a slightly different form in the online historical fiction journal *The Copperfield Review* (Winter 2000/1). The working title for the whole novel at these stages was still *The Shifting Surface of Desire*.

Brian Howell

*The Dance of Geometry:* Books Consulted

Svetlana Alpers: *The Art of Describing: Dutch Art in the Seventeenth Century* (1983)
Anthony Bailey: *A View of Delft, Vermeer then and now* (2001)
Albert Blankert, John Michael Montias, Gilles Aillaud: *Vermeer* (1988)
Lawrence Gowing: *Vermeer* (1952, 1997)
Donald Haks and Marie Christine van der Sman (eds): *Dutch Society in the Age of Vermeer* (1996)
Martin Kemp: *The Science of Art* (1990)
Balthasar de Monconys: *Journal de voyage de Monsieur de Monconys* (1665–6)
John Michael Montias: *Vermeer and His Milieu* (1989)
John Nash: *Vermeer* (1991)
Simon Schama: *The Embarrassment of Riches* (1987)
Edward Snow: *A Study of Vermeer* (1994, revised and enlarged edition)
Philip Steadman: *Vermeer's Camera* (2001)
P.T.A. Swillens: *Johannes Vermeer, Painter of Delft* (1950)
Hans Vredeman de Vries: *Perspective* (1604–5)
Arthur K. Wheelock, Jr, (ed): *Johannes Vermeer* (exhibition catalogue, 1995)
Arthur K. Wheelock, Jr: *Vermeer and the Art of Painting* (1995)
Arthur K. Wheelock, Jr: *Perspective, Optics, and Delft Artists around 1650* (1977)

# About the Author

*Brian Howell*

Brian Howell was born in London in 1961 and has lived in Germany, Hungary, and the Czech Republic. He currently lives in Japan with his wife and two children. His short stories have appeared regularly since 1990 in publications such as *Stand, Critical Quarterly, Panurge, The European,* and *Neonlit:The Time Out Book of New Writing*.

A fascination with Dutch seventeenth-century painting, a strong interest in cinema and photography, and the influence of the different cultures and languages with which he has been involved have often informed Howell's fiction. *The Dance of Geometry* is his first novel.

*The fonts used in the book are from the Garamond and
Frutiger families*